Praise for
BEN BROOKS

'Brilliant, brilliant, brilliant . . . A true gift for a reader'
Just Imagine

'A warm-hearted and magical adventure'
Armadillo Magazine

'A satisfying mix of quirky humour and all-action adventure
in a tale about the power of friends'
Sunday Express S Magazine

' . . . a laugh out loud book that pushes all senses of the
imagination to their limits. It is a masterpiece of creativity
and empathy rolled into one big feelgood tale'
ReadingZone

'A wonderful fantasy story'
The Times – Children's Book of the Week

'Brooks, known for his *Stories for Boys Who Dare to Be Different*
books, brings intellectual rigour and great imaginative power
to his first foray into fiction'
Financial Times

THE
DRAGON
ON
THE TRAIN

ALSO BY BEN BROOKS

Fiction

The Greatest Inventor

The Impossible Boy

Non-Fiction

Not All Heroes Wear Capes

Stories for Boys Who Dare to be Different

Stories for Boys Who Dare to be Different 2

Stories for Kids Who Dare to be Different

You Don't Have to be Loud: A Quiet Kid's Guide

to Being Heard

BEN BROOKS

THE DRAGON ON THE TRAIN

Quercus

QUERCUS CHILDREN'S BOOKS

First published in Great Britain in 2023 by Hodder & Stoughton Limited

1 3 5 7 9 10 8 6 4 2

Text copyright © Ben Brooks, 2023

Illustrations copyright © George Ermos, 2023

The moral rights of the author and illustrator have been asserted.

A CIP catalogue record for this book is available from the British Library.

ISBN 978 1 786 54190 1

Typeset in Minion Pro

Printed and bound by Clays Ltd, Elcograf S.p.A.

The paper and board used in this book are made from wood
from responsible sources.

Quercus Children's Books
An imprint of Hachette Children's Group
Part of Hodder & Stoughton Limited
Carmelite House
50 Victoria Embankment
London EC4Y 0DZ

An Hachette UK Company
www.hachette.co.uk

www.hachettechildrens.co.uk

For Nan.
And for her nan too.

1

Sixteen days after Grandma Ellen died, Elliot found a ticket under his pillow.

This ticket wasn't anything like the scrappy paper bus tickets that accumulated in the pockets of his school trousers. This ticket was printed on heavy, ocean-coloured card, and filled with ornate letters that wove in and out of each other like tangled headphones.

The ticket read:

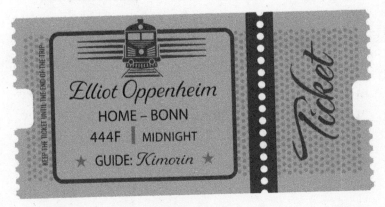

Elliot Oppenheim
HOME – BONN
444F ┃ MIDNIGHT
★ GUIDE: *Kimorin* ★

KEEP THE TICKET UNTIL THE END OF THE TRIP.

Ticket

Elliot stared at the ticket in the dim light of his bedroom, still half-asleep. The only thing on it that made any sense was his own name. What was it a ticket for, and who had left it there?

The sound of Mum's footsteps pattered up the stairs. Whatever the ticket meant, he didn't want his mum taking it away before he'd had time to work out what 'Kimorin' or 'Bonn' meant. Elliot hurriedly stuffed the ticket back under his pillow and rearranged himself to look as though he'd just woken up.

Mum threw open the curtains, flooding the room with pale April light. Outside, the few spindly trees that stood guard over their garden were dressed in preparation for the spring. The tips of their branches had squeezed out vivid, kite-shaped leaves and a sparkling sheen of dew coated the patchy lawn.

'Morning, sleepyhead,' she said.

Elliot buried his face in the crook of his elbow to keep out the sudden glare. The world outside of his duvet was too cold and too bright. He had no interest in joining it.

Mum asked how Elliot was feeling. In response, he mumbled nothing in particular. Elliot still wasn't entirely sure how he was feeling. He was sad, he knew that, but this was a different kind of sadness to the time he'd been sick during a violin exam, or the day he'd accidentally dropped all of his pocket money through a sewer grate. It was like comparing a grass snake to a velociraptor – a member of the same family, perhaps, but almost unrecognisable.

Mum perched on the end of Elliot's bed, freckly hands folded in her lap. Her long, ginger hair gathered into a pool on his duvet. She was dressed in her work clothes: a cartoon-covered shirt, a yellow tie, and a baggy pair of grey trousers. Elliot's mum, Anita Oppenheim, worked for the local newspaper. She wrote articles about local protests and lost dogs and people who had lived to be a hundred years old.

'I think it's best if you go to school today,' she told Elliot. 'The sooner we start getting back to normal, the better.'

Elliot had known she was going to say that, but it didn't make it any easier to hear. The week before, school had been closed for half-term and the week before that, his mum had let Elliot pretend to be too sick to get out of bed.

And now things were supposed to go back to normal.

He didn't want to 'go back to normal' because

nothing felt normal. Everything felt the opposite of normal. Going to school when Grandma Ellen had just died would be like eating a bacon roll during a hurricane or trying to sleep while your house was on fire. How exactly was he supposed to carry on as normal when nothing would ever be normal again?

'Well?' said Mum. 'What do you think? You've got violin today and I know Mrs Lancet will be excited to see you.'

Knowing it would be useless to argue, Elliot heaved himself into a sitting position and rubbed the moon-dust out of his eyes.

He nodded.

Mum thanked him, kissed him between the eyes, and left. Her smell stayed behind for a few seconds after she'd gone, honey-nut cereal and printer ink hanging in the air.

Elliot hadn't wanted to say it in front of her, but there was no way he was going to his violin lesson. There was no way he was even touching his violin. It had been two weeks since Grandma Ellen had passed away in her sleep, at the prison-shaped hospital on the edge of town, and since then Elliot had not listened to a single piece of music. (If he accidentally heard music, in a shop or coming out of a passing car, he shouted nonsense in his head to try and block it out. Most of the time, this nonsense went something along the lines of: *AH FOR NAH GRAH or BAH FAR LOG LOO*.)

For any other child, avoiding music might not have meant much. For Elliot Oppenheim, it was huge.

Generally speaking, the only time Elliot didn't wear headphones was when he was playing violin, and the only time he wasn't playing violin was when he was wearing headphones. Since Grandma Ellen had died, he had done neither. And he had no plans to.

Almost all of the music he liked had been shown to him by his nan.

She liked the lilting folk of The Dubliners, the doom-laden guitars of Slipknot, the bubbling synths of Kraftwerk. She liked music written hundreds of years ago and she liked music written yesterday. She liked music that, to Elliot, barely even sounded like music.

Together, the two of them would spend hours listening to songs, watching music videos and learning duets. Grandma Ellen played the cello, which she said was the boxer of the string family. The violin was a ballerina. Sometimes when they played together, Elliot would imagine a bloody-nosed fighter and a sinewy dancer chasing each other in circles.

On the bus to school, Elliot sat with his forehead pressed against the window. Even without his headphones on, he was oblivious to what was going on around him. He didn't hear Priyanka and Lucy arguing over which rapper was the best rapper. He didn't see Lewis pulling apart his ham sandwich and launching its halves in the direction of the driver. And he didn't smell Elita burping 'All Things Bright and Beautiful' with the force of three hastily sunk Diet Cokes.

At registration, Miss Cliff had to call his name three times before he answered. When he did, she gave him a strange little smile, as though she understood a little of how he was feeling, which he very much doubted.

Elliot sat through the first lessons in a kind of fog, fidgeting with things he found buried in his pencil case and staring out of cloudy windows.

Breaktime started at 11 a.m. and by 11.01 a.m., Elliot was sitting in a toilet cubicle, hugging his knees to his chest. He didn't know how not to think about it, to not think about Grandma Ellen. How was he supposed to concentrate on the Tudors or how gravity works when his grandma had just . . . well, gone?

Gone.

It was a word that both made sense and made no sense at all. Elliot knew that goldfish died, and cats died, and dogs died. On some level, he even knew that grandmas died. He just hadn't quite believed that *his* grandma could die.

And now she had.

And in two days' time, he was supposed to put on an incredibly uncomfortable suit and sit in a church while relatives he barely knew would talk about how much they missed her. He couldn't bear the thought. In fact, he'd decided that he wasn't going to go. There was no way that he was going to stand in a cold, draughty church, crying in front of a coffin while he tried to sing hymns. No, thank you – he could think of far better places to cry. He would find a small, dark place to hide until it was all over.

There was a faint knock on the door of the toilet cubicle.

'Oppenheim?' said a voice. 'You in there?'

'What do you want?' answered Elliot.

'I'm supposed to tell you that you're late for your violin lesson.' There was a small burp. 'This is Lewis, by the way. Mrs Lancet sent me.'

Elliot gulped. 'I'm not going,' he said. 'Tell her I'm not going.'

'She said you might say that,' Lewis said. 'And I'm meant to tell you that you're supposed to go anyway.'

'I'm not going – just leave me alone!' Elliot shouted, surprising himself.

There was a brief pause.

'Whatever,' said Lewis. 'You don't have to shout, you know. No wonder you don't have any friends.'

Elliot heard the door slam and he felt something heavy fall through his chest. With the effort of trying not to cry, his nose started to run. He closed his eyes and watched purple planets spinning on the insides of his eyelids.

Lewis was right: Elliot didn't have any friends. No one at school had ever really made sense to him. Most of the boys liked talking about football or cars or PlayStation games where you shot people in the face, none of which Elliot knew anything about. He got on with some of the girls in his class a little better, but the older they'd got, the less they wanted to speak to him, as if a rule had slowly appeared out of nowhere saying that they weren't meant to be friends.

Grandma Ellen had been his best friend.

Elliot knew that your grandma wasn't supposed to be your best friend, but it wasn't like he hadn't tried to make friends. He didn't like football, didn't own a PlayStation, and got incredibly sick during car journeys. The prospect of cars that could go much faster than normal cars did not appeal to him in the slightest. And, at the end of the day, he would rather spend time with Grandma Ellen.

Elliot stayed in the toilet cubicle until a teacher came and led him to geography. The teacher didn't tell him off, which surprised Elliot. They did, however, make it clear that hiding in the toilet was no longer allowed and he was expected to attend lessons like everyone else.

Miss Cliff spent that afternoon talking about how the ice in the Arctic was melting. Elliot spent it staring at a black smudge on the wall.

As soon as Elliot got home, he rushed upstairs and climbed into bed. He felt exhausted, as though he'd spent the day running from polar bears rather than learning about them. He decided that he wouldn't go back to school. Not tomorrow. Or the day after that. Or any of the days after that. From now on, he would live in his bed. He wouldn't go out into the world when everyone acted like nothing was wrong.

And if people kept trying to make him go to violin lessons, he'd smash his violin. Then there was no way they could make him go.

People die! he wanted to shout. *And not just any people, but the people you like most!*

Yet teachers still expected him to care about countries he'd never visit and maths problems about made-up people buying made-up apples from made-up shops. Had they never heard about dying? How could they keep walking around with smiles on their faces? How could they still listen to any music at all?

When she got back from work, Elliot's mum made dinner and brought it upstairs.

'It's lasagne,' she said gently. 'Your favourite.'

Elliot didn't say anything. He kept his eyes closed and tried to make his breaths as long and deep as possible, so that she'd think he was sleeping and leave him alone. This was a tactic he'd been perfecting for years.

Mum tucked a lock of loose hair behind Elliot's ear. 'How about I leave it on the floor by your bed and when you get hungry, you can help yourself?' she asked.

Elliot didn't make a sound. He knew that if he admitted he was awake, his mum would start asking how his day had gone, and he'd have to tell her he didn't go to his violin lesson, which would mean talking about a lot of things that he really didn't want to talk about.

'There's something else,' said his mum. 'Something I think might cheer you up.' Elliot held his breath. Whatever it was, he really couldn't imagine that it was going to make him feel in the least bit better. Unless, he thought, she was about to tell him that there had been a big mistake and Grandma Ellen was fine and everything was going to go back to how it was.

'We were going through a few of Grandma's old things earlier today and we found a tape in an envelope. On the envelope, it said it was for you.'

She paused as if expecting some sort of reaction but was met with silence. 'Do you want me to put it on?' asked Mum.

Still, Elliot didn't say anything. He didn't want to hear any music, especially not anything from Grandma Ellen. Music didn't work for him any more. It didn't make him feel happy or excited or free or strong. It just made him feel sad. All of it. No matter what song was playing or who it was being played by.

'I'll put it on,' said Mum. 'Then I'll leave you alone so you can have a doze.'

Part of Elliot wanted to jump up and shout at his mother not to play the tape. Another part of him would do anything to avoid having to explain that he wanted to stop playing the violin. He could picture the disappointment clouding her face. He could imagine just how upset she'd be that not only would she never hear Grandma Ellen play music again, she'd never hear him again either.

After pressing play on the stereo, Mum left the room.

The first few notes of the tape rose out of the speakers and into the air.

Elliot tried to force himself off the bed to stop it, but he couldn't move. It was as though some invisible force was keeping him pinned to the bed. No matter how much he wanted to get up, his body seemed to have decided it didn't want to listen to him any more.

The music played.

Elliot balled his hands into fists and pressed them against his ears. *AH FOR NAH GRAH*, he thought-shouted. *BAH FAR LOG LOO*. This barely had any effect at all. The music seeped past his fingers and into his head.

It was not a piece of music he'd ever heard before. Elliot quickly realised that whatever was playing, Grandma Ellen must have written it herself. She'd once written a lot of music, recording it all on an old, silver karaoke machine that she'd bought at a car boot sale. But the older she got, the less she wrote. She said that she wanted to listen to as much of other people's music as possible, and that meant there was no time for her to sit around making up her own.

The song began with a simple loop of four notes. Without trying, Elliot could pick them out of the air:

The stern bowing of the cello carried Elliot out of his bedroom. His breaths grew fast and shallow and the bed under his body hummed. Elliot closed his eyes. He drove his fists harder against his ears. He felt the irresistible pull of sounds on his thoughts.

It was as though the music was asking him questions he didn't want to answer. Could he picture a lonely mountain? Did he wish the day was over? Could he remember that Sunday afternoon on the beach when Grandma Ellen sang so loudly that every single bird disappeared into the clouds? What was he going to do now she wasn't here? Was it okay to cry now?

The music asked him questions and demanded answers. The four notes danced in and out of each other, before being joined by four more that climbed each other like acrobats. It felt as though Elliot was in a boat on a raging sea. The water beneath his bed rocked him back and forth. His eyes filled with hot tears. For the first time since he'd been given the news about his grandma, he let himself explode. He let himself cry, loud and ugly. He let himself scream, face buried in his pillow. And he let his body thrash madly on his mattress like a fish out of water.

As he cried and screamed and shook, the music played on around him.

Before he knew it, Elliot was asleep. Deep asleep. Far deeper than he'd slept in weeks. It was a heavy, dreamless sleep, which came as a welcome relief from a painful day.

But it didn't last.

Around five minutes to midnight, Elliot was woken by a loud snuffling sound. If he'd had to guess, with his eyes closed, what the sound was, he might have gone for 'dog with its head stuck in the biscuit jar' or 'washing machine filled with spaghetti'.

He opened his eyes.

It wasn't a dog.

Something much larger than that was eating his food.

2

*E*lliot shrieked and rolled backwards off his bed,
landing with a thump on the carpet. The creature
stuffing its face in his dinner was . . . a small
dragon. (Well, small for a dragon, but large for
something that appeared without warning in your
bedroom.)

It had a sticky-out belly, dull scales and a tail that
flicked back and forth behind its head. A glass lantern
that cast long diamonds of yellow light across Elliot's
carpet hung from the end of its tail. On its head, the
dragon wore a battered straw hat that sat at a jaunty
angle. The hat wobbled precariously above a pair of
electric-blue eyes as the creature ravenously devoured
the lasagne that Elliot's mum had left out.

'Who are you?' blurted Elliot, peering above the
opposite end of his bed. 'What do you want?'

The creature lifted its head from the food. Specks

of meat and gooey strings of cheese hung from its mouth.

'Kimorin,' replied the creature, licking its lips. 'Lasagne.'

Elliot lowered his trembling fists. 'Kimorin?' he said. That name was written on the ticket he'd found under his pillow that morning.

The creature nodded, wiping its mouth with the back of a claw. 'Sound familiar? It should do. I'm to be your guardian! Only, I turn up here to find you out like a light, and a perfectly good plate of restaurant-grade Italian chow turnin' to bug food.'

'I've already got a guardian,' said Elliot. 'And she doesn't sleep very well so you should probably go now.'

Kimorin started to shake with laughter, his scales rippling and glinting in the beams of lantern light. 'Not a legal guardian,' said the creature, as if it were the most obvious thing in the world. 'I ain't tryin' to adopt you, Olio. I'm your guide for the duration of your journey, that's all.'

'My name's actually Elliot—'

'That's what I said, Olio.'

'—and I'm not going anywhere,' protested Elliot.

'I'm going to sleep and then I'm going to live in my bed.'

Kimorin scratched his head. 'Are you sure?'

'Positive,' said Elliot.

The dragon raised the darkened patches of scales above his eyes where a human might have had eyebrows. 'So you ain't got a ticket?'

Elliot swallowed, wondering whether he ought to lie. Would the creature go away if he pretended he had no ticket? Somehow, he doubted it. 'Yes,' admitted Elliot. 'I have a ticket, but I didn't ask for it and I don't know what it is. If you want, you can have it.' Elliot hurriedly climbed back on to his bed, grabbed the ticket from under his pillow, and held it out in the direction of the dragon. 'Here.'

At that, Kimorin leaped up on to Elliot's bed and flashed a smile crammed with blunt, slightly yellow teeth. 'Nobody asks for a ticket; that's not how things work,' he said. 'A ticket is like a rainstorm – sometimes you just get one. And no matter how many lasagnes you ignore, it won't go away. This is important stuff, Olio. Someone wanted you to have it.'

'But what's it a ticket for?' asked Elliot, deciding that convincing the dragon to pronounce his name properly was the least of his worries.

Kimorin took a couple of shuffling steps towards Elliot, who pressed himself as far back against the wall as he could. The closer the creature came, the faster his heart went, and Elliot realised that as it moved, the dragon left behind black, star-shaped footprints on the bed. He briefly wondered how he was going to explain that to his mum.

'It's for *The Night Train*,' said Kimorin. 'Don't it say that on it?'

'No,' said Elliot, turning the ticket over in his hands as though more words were going to appear. 'What's *The Night Train*?'

'So many questions!' said the little dragon. 'Now, I've got two questions for you, Olio.' Elliot swallowed. 'Have you heard of trains?'

'Yes,' said Elliot.

'And have you heard of the night?'

'Of course,' said Elliot.

'Well then, I ain't entirely sure what it is you're findin' so impossibly mysterious. You goin' dressed like that? 'Cos we're about to leave. Unless you'd rather stay here and get munched up by a Hush-Hush, which I most definitely do not recommend.' Elliot opened his mouth to speak but Kimorin had already reached forward and placed a single, surprisingly soft claw against his lips to keep him from saying anything else. 'Now don't you ask what a Hush-Hush is, because I've had it up to my earholes with questions for now, and we've got stuff to do.'

At that, the wardrobe against the back wall of Elliot's room started to rock from side to side, as though there was something trapped inside of it, desperately fighting to get out. Needless to say, the wardrobe had never acted in such a way before, and Elliot felt a combination of terrified, confused and like it was very possible that he was dreaming.

'There, we have our way out,' announced Kimorin eagerly, bouncing off the bed and standing before the trembling piece of furniture. 'Or in, I s'pose, dependin' on how you look at it.'

Elliot had no idea what was going on.

It was only his old, lime-green wardrobe that his mum had found on top of a skip two streets away. This was how they found most of their furniture: they took in what others threw out. It meant their house looked a lot like an antiques shop. There were ancient, broken grandfather clocks and stained rugs and tiny porcelain cats. There were pewter mugs the size of heads and half-unravelled rugs and faded oil paintings of farmers standing by towering stacks of yellow hay. Best of all, there was an old upright piano, so out of tune that anything you played on it sounded like the soundtrack to a horror film.

Elliot much preferred his home to houses where everything was the same colour. He'd once visited Ryan Gale's bungalow for a birthday party the entire class had been invited to. Every single wall, decoration and piece of furniture had been the colour of eggshells. It had made Elliot feel as though he was walking through the most boring alien planet ever to have been discovered.

Elliot realised he'd stopped breathing when Kimorin announced that the train was due to arrive any second and they ought to get moving. The dragon gave the boy an excited nudge with one of his wings, lifted his lantern and leaped off the bed. He stood eagerly next to the wardrobe, hopping from one foot to the other.

Hugging a pillow to his chest, Elliot tried scrunching his eyes shut, as though that would return everything to normal.

The green doors of the wardrobe flew open.

'Drop the pillow, Olio,' said Kimorin. 'It's time to go.'

3

It was raining inside Elliot's wardrobe. A kind of peaceful, steady spring rain that dripped from the tips of leaves and trickled along the gutters of the small train station. The station was little more than a short platform beside a set of tracks, under a domed glass roof that crackled with the falling raindrops.

Through the glass ceiling, there were stars. More stars than Elliot had ever seen. They clustered together like bees in the swirling purple sky. These stars seemed closer than the stars Elliot was used to. He felt like if he stood on his tiptoes and reached between the branches of the trees, he'd be able to pull one out of the sky.

Strolling up and down the platform in a neat, emerald-green suit was a man far taller than anyone Elliot knew. The man wore a spotless red felt coat over a bulging waistcoat. A blue cap glistening with gold

24

thread sat perched on his head and a gleaming silver whistle hung around his neck.

'Home!' the conductor called out, waving a wooden paddle. 'Alight here for Home!'

No one, it seemed, wanted to get off.

Kimorin nudged Elliot forward and the two of them stepped through the wardrobe.

The tall man recognised the little dragon. He broke into a smile as the creature approached.

'You managed to locate your young charge after all?' asked the tall man, crouching slightly to get a better look at Elliot.

'Oh, I got him in the end,' said Kimorin. 'He was nappin' next to a lasagne goldmine, practically beggin' to be ate up by a Hush-Hush. Ain't that right, Olio?'

'My name's Elliot,' said Elliot. 'And I don't know what a Hush-Hush is.'

'Careful,' whispered Kimorin to the tall man, shielding his mouth with half a wing as though he was telling a secret. 'Or he'll start askin' you questions. And once he starts, he keeps goin'.'

'Pleased to meet you, Elliot.' The tall man lowered his face even further, so that he was practically bent in half, and he offered a giant hand to Elliot to shake. Not wanting to be rude, Elliot took hold of one of the fingers and moved it up and down. The tall man winked. 'No need to worry about the Hushes, little sir – you're with the finest dragon guardian either side of Lake Largo.'

Elliot nodded, dazed, as he took in the train. It was made up of so many carriages that he couldn't see either end. Glowing panes of glass stretched endlessly in both directions, casting shadows on the platform of people clinking mugs, clutching cards and passing out tiny biscuits and segments of fruit. He could see the twitching shadows of instruments too: flutes and mandolins and circular bodhrán drums, with the shadows of hands flying up and down them.

The train was like no train Elliot had ever seen, except in the old detective films his nan would watch on Sunday afternoons. Its panels had been delicately painted by hand, with ornate golden borders and curling letters and numbers. Gleaming brass handles were fixed to the doors and glass orbs of orange light hung over the windows. The air around the train smelled of dusty smoke and rain and fresh soil.

There was music coming from somewhere above everything, music that Elliot felt more in his fingertips than in his ears. A kind of faint, metallic twinkle that sparkled over a deep and distant beat. Elliot wasn't sure if he was imagining it, but he thought he caught those four notes from the tape.

'On you get, chaps,' said the conductor, flinging open a door and motioning for Elliot and Kimorin to climb on board.

Though Kimorin hurriedly bounced up the steps, Elliot paused before getting on and looked around. To his surprise, there was no sign of his wardrobe on the platform.

Elliot knew then that he had no choice but to go on, that whatever was happening was already happening, but a very large part of him wished he wasn't about to embark on a night-time adventure with an impatient dragon. Grandma Ellen was still gone, and the thought hung over Elliot like a raincloud. He wasn't in the mood for going on adventures; he was in the mood for going nowhere at all. He was in the mood for lying curled up in bed with his back to the world.

Standing with his hand gripping the railing, Elliot leaned forward to look into the train and swallowed.

Kimorin reappeared, his head poking around the corner. Elliot thought the creature was going to tell him off again but instead it gave him the same sad smile that Miss Cliff had given him earlier that day.

'Can I give you a little advice, Olio?' said Kimorin. Elliot shrugged. 'No one ever thought themselves happy. Doesn't happen. It would be like thinkin' a tiger into existence. If you could think yourself happy, there wouldn't be no need for happy songs or jigsaw puzzles or knock-knock jokes. What does that mean for you and me? It means we ain't about to stand around thinkin' when we're sad – we're gonna get on that train and see where it takes us.'

'You mean you don't know where it goes?' asked Elliot.

The train let out a piercing whistle.

'Please stand back from the platform!' bellowed the tall man. 'The train is now departing!'

Kimorin reached out a claw to Elliot. 'Course I know where it goes,' he said. 'It goes wherever your ticket says it's s'posed to go. If you get on, we can take a look.'

The boy sighed, took hold of his claw and climbed aboard the train.

He found himself standing in a surprisingly spacious hallway. The floor was carpeted with a deep layer of soft red. On the wood-panelled walls, framed pictures hung in wonky rows. A few were maps of the stars, which Elliot recognised, but most of the others were photographs of people holding instruments. In one, a lanky, gentle-looking woman in a top hat clutched a saxophone in a room filled with smoke. In another, a young boy stood alone on a mountaintop, holding a tin whistle to his lips. Most of the people in the photographs were playing with their eyes shut, oblivious to their surroundings.

'Let's get another look at that ticket, then,' said the dragon.

Elliot pulled the thick piece of card out of his pocket and passed it over.

Kimorin scanned it quickly before waving it triumphantly in front of Elliot's face. 'Did you read this thing at all? We're going to Bonn, Olio, it says so right there.'

'Bonn's a place? Where is it?'

'Who cares?' said the dragon. 'We ain't drivin'. Most important question is: where are we s'posed to be now?' Kimorin studied the ticket again and glanced down the carriageway, nodding. 'That ain't so bad,' he said. 'Pretty good seats, as a matter of fact. I've sat in worse.'

The door that led into 444F was a sliding oak panel fitted with round portholes. Inside, the cabin was a cosy space with four seats, a low wooden table, and a pale light that emanated from a lamp resembling the kind of hat someone might wear to a wedding. There were woollen blankets folded over the backs of the seats and, above them, brass luggage racks waited for suitcases. Heavy, red-fabric curtains were pinned at either side of a large window that looked out on to a forest crowded with spiny trees.

The boy and the dragon took seats opposite each other.

The engine rumbled to life.

The curtains fluttered.

As the train pulled away from the platform, Elliot sat with his knees tucked underneath him and his face pressed against the window. Drops of rain raced each other to the bottom of the glass, blurring his view. He saw the orange light of the train's lamps glancing off endless armies of gnarled trunks.

'Be right back,' said Kimorin, bouncing out of the door.

And Elliot was left alone in the cabin.

A train suddenly felt like one of the worst places he could have ended up. Not because he didn't like trains, but because he'd spent so much time on them with Grandma Ellen. Some weekends, when his mum had to work, Grandma Ellen would turn up at his house unannounced and tell him to put on a coat, then meet her in the car. They'd go to the train station, look at the departures board and pick a destination at random. Grandma Ellen loved trains almost as much as she loved music. She kept notes about their journeys in a purpose-bought notepad with lines so small you could barely read the writing squeezed in between them. These notes were used to match songs to stretches of countryside, so that she could remember what they'd listened to while going past a certain supermarket, tumbledown cottage or field packed with bored-looking cows.

On each journey, Grandma Ellen would encourage Elliot to notice how certain pieces of music changed the way he felt about the landscapes they were passing through.

Do the trees look different when you're hearing Vivaldi? she would ask. *What about if Iron Maiden are thrashing about in your ears?*

Does the music make you feel happy or sleepy or hungry or nothing at all?

How, she always wanted to know, *does music change how we see the world?*

Most of the time, Elliot liked the songs Grandma Ellen chose to play through the old pair of earphones they shared. Sometimes the music she played him was too weird or sad or old for him to really get into, but it helped that she'd always let him get a hot chocolate from the food trolley. That was one benefit of having your nan as your best friend: she was almost always willing to buy you a hot chocolate.

Elliot didn't have any brothers or sisters. He'd asked his mum why not and she'd told him that she used up all her love on him. Sometimes, this felt incredibly unfair, but when he was spending time with Grandma Ellen, it didn't bother him so much. He had someone to do stuff with, and it didn't really matter that her hair was white, and she didn't understand YouTube and, sometimes, if she laughed too hard, her teeth fell out.

This was what Elliot was thinking about when Kimorin reappeared, holding two mugs and humming a jazz riff under his breath. The lantern on his tail swung from side to side. He passed one of the cups to Elliot and returned to his seat on the other side of the table. For a while, neither of them said anything. The downpour seemed to be gathering pace, beating louder and louder on the roof of the train, like a person who wanted to be let inside.

The trees outside shivered in the rain.

Gusts of wind whipped water across the windows.

'Drink up,' said the dragon. 'It'll make you feel a lot better, that will.'

Elliot took a sip from his mug. It tasted exactly like the tea they had at home. The dragon hadn't asked but, somehow, he'd known to put one and a half sugars in, along with an extra splash of milk.

'How's that goin' down?'

'I don't know,' said Elliot. The tea had reminded him of his mum, who drank exactly nine cups every day. He'd been so busy thinking about Grandma Ellen that he hadn't paused to think how his mum would feel when she woke up and found his bed empty. Of course, she might be so busy with work that she wouldn't even realise he was gone. She was always hunting for stories, looking for the breakthrough that would mean she could get a better job at one of the big newspapers.

The dragon chuckled. 'Now,' he said. 'I spoke to our humble driver about where and what Bonn might be. You'll be pleased to know that she told me to keep my trunk out of her business.' Kimorin leaped on to his seat and pointed dramatically to his nose. 'I ask you, Olio, does this look like a trunk? This is a nose, same as yours. I ain't an elephant and I ain't an aardvark.'

'I need to get home,' said Elliot, not particularly interested in whether the dragon had a trunk or not. 'If Mum wakes up and I'm not there, she'll be scared and she'll call the police and everyone will go out looking for me. She's already sad enough as it is, and she has so much on at work.'

'Olio, do you have absolutely no faith in me as your temporary custodian?' Elliot didn't know how to answer that. He stared blankly at the dragon, before shrugging, and turning his eyes back towards the blurry scenery scrolling past the window. 'Course no one's lookin' for you. They won't even realise you're gone.'

'But if we don't get back, Mum will come to check on me and she'll see I'm not there and she'll be scared.' Elliot set his mug down on the table and crossed his arms. 'It was stupid to come with you,' he said. 'I don't know who you are, and I don't want to be on a train. If you don't take me home right now, I'm going to call the police.'

Kimorin sighed. It was a big, weary sigh, the kind you might give when someone's just said something incredibly silly. He rolled off his seat, tottered across the carriage, and jumped up next to Elliot. The dragon was about a head taller than the boy. His eyes, Elliot noticed for the first time, were like the inside of a kaleidoscope; if you turned your head, old patterns came apart to form new ones.

'Olio, what did you do today?' Kimorin asked slowly, like a maths teacher explaining that two ducks plus three ducks equals five ducks.

Elliot stared at the dragon impatiently. 'How does that have anything to do with anything?'

'Listen. Maybe, if you stop givin' me questions

instead of answers, you might find somethin' out.'

Elliot huffed. 'Today, I went to school,' he said.

Kimorin leaned in closer. 'And then?'

'And then I don't know. I ate a KitKat on the way home?'

A look of horror spread across Kimorin's face. 'You ate a cat?'

'A KitKat,' said Elliot. 'It's a kind of sweet.'

'And it's cat-flavoured?'

'No, it's chocolate-flavoured.'

'But after you ate this chocolate-flavoured cat, you got into your bed?'

'Yes. I got into my bed and fell asleep until you woke me up and made me get on this train.'

'Right.' Kimorin clambered over Elliot until he was standing on the table, facing the rain-spattered window. With a single deep and slightly fiery breath, the dragon misted up the entire pane of glass. He used the tip of a claw to write into the fog.

First, Kimorin wrote 'school', then 'chocolate cat', then 'bed'. He connected them all with arrows, like this:

SCHOOL → CHOCOLATE CAT → BED

'Does that look about right?' he asked. Elliot nodded. 'Course it does, because you are a human person, and human persons have a very simple way of lookin' at time.'

'What does that mean?'

'Human persons only understand time as it happens to them. They start as small babies, then turn into adults, then disappear. Always in that order. Because of that, they assume that time only moves forward. But if they paid a little more attention, they'd realise that ain't true at all.'

'Isn't it?' asked Elliot.

'No, Olio, it ain't. Not necessarily, at least. Take the example of a river. You can float with the current of the river, as most of you humans do, all headin' in the same direction. Or you can swim against the current, though that'll leave you knackered. But your third option, which many seem to forget, is to climb out of the river entirely.' Kimorin took in Elliot's confused face. '"But how do you climb out of the river?" he's about to ask me. Listen, I ain't going to answer that because you already know the answer – you just have to think about it a little.'

Elliot had no idea what the dragon was talking

about. 'I already know how to climb out of a river?'

'Out of a metaphorical river,' corrected Kimorin.

'But I don't know what a metaphorical river is,' said Elliot.

'Well, it's like a river,' said Kimorin. 'But it's somethin' else. In this case, it's time. How do you climb out of time?'

Elliot scratched his head. 'Go to sleep?' he asked.

Kimorin made a loud buzzer sound. 'Incorrect!' he bellowed. 'Try again.'

'I don't really feel like games,' said Elliot, turning away from the dragon and back towards the window. He pressed his fingertip to one of the raindrops and traced its route as it fell. 'I still really need to go home. Could you ask the driver if we could go back?'

'Does your ticket say "back" on it, Olio? Or does it say "Bonn"?'

Elliot was beginning to grow frustrated with the dragon. 'We haven't made it very far. If we turn around now, it'll take no time at all.'

Kimorin shook his head. 'Trains don't turn around, Olio, even you should know that. And I'm not talkin' to that driver again. Who knows what she'll call me this time. A tadpole? A donkey? A wiener schnitzel?

Dragons do not have trunks; we have noses. I should think that was plain as a cheese sandwich, even to human persons.'

Kimorin continued to ramble about noses and trunks until the train came to a stop.

Through the window, Elliot could see that they were on the outskirts of a village. The rain had slowed almost to a stop and the night sky over the cluster of buildings was clear. Though it was difficult to make much out in the darkness, the houses seemed to Elliot to have unusual shapes. They weren't the low, squashed-together brick buildings of his town. These houses were high, their roofs sloped steeply into tall peaks like the turrets of castles. Black wooden beams criss-crossed the walls so that the structures looked like drawings that had been coloured in.

The dragon leaped off his seat and flung open the door of cabin 444F. 'You comin' or what?' he said.

'Do I have to?' asked Elliot, who hadn't been entirely convinced by all the talk of time and rivers.

'Course you don't.' Kimorin planted a paw on each of his hips and twitched the tips of his wings. 'You're welcome to sit around here on your lonesome and find out for yourself what a Hush-Hush is.'

Grumbling, Elliot took one last look around the cosy train carriage and followed his dragon guardian out into the night.

4

The station was completely deserted. There was no one in the ticket hatch, no one at the control station and no one waiting on the benches. Elliot also noticed that none of the other passengers had got off the train.

A stone building was all that kept watch over the tracks. On its wall hung a clock, its hands frozen at 8.15.

Birds gossiped on the platform roof. Two black cats lay below a bench, their front legs stretched out like sphinxes.

As Elliot took in his surroundings, *The Night Train* thundered away, leaving behind a trail of twisting smoke in the sky. With it, the music of his grandma's song faded.

But it didn't leave behind silence, as he'd been expecting. Another song was playing in the night. This song was curling up from the village, its notes the clear, round, porcelain notes of a piano. The new music sounded almost familiar to Elliot. Almost, but not quite. Like meeting the brother or sister of someone you've known for a long time.

'Right,' said the dragon. 'Apparently this is Bonn. I expect we're s'posed to follow the music. That's usually where the fun is, ain't it? Wherever the music's comin' from.'

Elliot shook his head.

'What's wrong?' said Kimorin. 'You got a worm in your earhole?'

Elliot shook his head again. 'No,' he said.

'Then why do you keep wigglin' your head about like that?'

'Because I don't want to be around any music.' Elliot looked up and down the platform. He shuffled over to a bench, crossed his arms and sat down. 'I'll just stay here and wait for the next train.'

'Your ticket ain't a return, Olio. If you want to go anywhere else, you'll be needin' another ticket. Now where do you s'pose they might come from?'

Elliot looked uncertainly around him at the deserted station. 'From a ticket machine?' he asked, even though there wasn't a single ticket machine – or any type of machine, for that matter – in sight.

'Nice try, Olio. But no. In my humble experience, the tickets tend to come from the same place as the music. So, if you're gonna get anywhere, we're gonna need to head towards the piano.'

Balling his hands into fists, Elliot let out a sudden roar of frustration. It shocked the birds off the platform and startled the little dragon.

'That feel better?' asked Kimorin after a moment.

Elliot shrugged. 'I don't know.'

'Up you get,' the dragon said. 'Let's go find you another ticket, Olio.'

Together, Elliot and Kimorin made their way along the winding path that led from the empty train station into the village. There were no lamp posts to light their way. The only guiding light came from the crescent moon, shining valiantly among the stars. Its white glow picked out the cobblestones of the unfamiliar streets.

Elliot stumbled a few times, not used to walking on such uneven ground. At home the roads were perfectly flat stretches of black tarmac. *Why would anyone build such a lumpy road?* he wondered. *Do they actually want people to fall over?*

The two of them came to a brief stop beside a fountain. Though it was filled with water, the fountain was still. Hundreds of coins glinted below the surface. Elliot wondered about all the wishes made by all the people who'd thrown away their money. Had any of them come true? He thought about how many times he must have wished on birthday cakes, tossed coins and stray eyelashes, blown off his nan's fingertips. All the wishes he'd ever made seemed so small and silly now.

The melody that they'd followed from the train station stopped for a brief moment before starting up again.

The dragon sniffed the air.

'There you are,' he muttered, chasing the music around a corner, with Elliot trying his best to keep up.

The dragon headed down a street lined with four-storey buildings that jostled for space as though they all wanted to be picked first for a team. Each of the buildings was fronted by a heavy-looking door and windows flanked by wooden shutters.

On each building, the wooden shutters were closed. The whole town seemed to be asleep.

The whole town except for one floor of one house, where the shutters were thrown open, spilling light out on to the cobbled street. This house was where Kimorin came to a halt. He stood a few steps away and motioned for Elliot to move closer.

'Don't be shy,' said Kimorin. 'Nobody's gonna see you.'

Once again, Elliot shook his head. He didn't want to look into the house or get any closer to the music.

'Best shake out those earworms quick if you want to get outta here,' the dragon told him.

Elliot sighed. He tensed every muscle in his body before hesitantly shuffling closer to the window. The glass was thick, warped and clouded with soot and dirt. Elliot pulled his hand up into his sleeve and used the end of his jumper to wipe a circle out of the muck. This gave him a clearer view of the sad living room.

Inside, the last embers of a fire were sparkling in a stone fireplace. A plain, frayed rug stretched itself over splintered wooden floorboards. The ceiling above was the stained brown colour of tissue paper that had been used to mop up spilled tea.

In the centre of the room, a very small boy sat on top of a stack of books in front of a piano. He couldn't have been more than seven years old, but it became clear that this boy was the one responsible for the music. This tiny boy was the one making that beautiful, complicated racket.

Elliot was amazed.

As though he could sense Elliot's eyes on him, the boy suddenly stopped playing.

The shadow of a man appeared out of nowhere, startling even Elliot.

He barked something at the boy in a language that Elliot couldn't understand. Though he didn't know the words, he knew the tone. The man was furious, and Elliot felt terrified, even from the other side of the glass. The boy's shoulders started to jerk up and down. He was crying.

'Does he have the tickets?' Elliot said, turning to Kimorin.

The dragon gestured for him to keep looking. The boy placed his tiny fingers on top of the keys. He looked at them as though he was afraid of what they might do. He lifted a hand to wipe a tear from his cheek, placed it back down again and stretched his fingers so wide that it reminded Elliot of seagulls unfolding their wings.

The man barked.

And the boy started to play.

The song that had led them into the town had only been a warm-up. This piece was as complicated as anything Elliot had ever seen his grandma play on her cello. It was a grand, boisterous piece of music that sounded like something that might herald the arrival of a wise but slightly terrifying king. The ruler of a kingdom where stone castles climbed through the clouds and bold knights chased each other through dark forests.

The boy played without even bothering to watch his hands, which flew up and down the keys like creatures he could barely control. He was so small compared to the instrument that his entire body rocked from side to side as he reached for the highest and lowest octaves on the piano.

'He's good,' whispered Elliot to his dragon guardian, as he stared at the boy in awe.

'Better than good, Olio,' said Kimorin. 'He's a genius.'

They continued to watch as the boy carried on

playing, his hands flying up and down the piano with a speed that made Elliot feel tired just watching it. The way the boy played piano reminded Elliot of the way his mother typed at a computer; both looked as though they were trying to use their fingers to dig for buried treasure.

During a difficult passage in the music, the boy fumbled a note, his tiny fingers failing to stretch far enough to catch a high key. The giant of a man standing behind him brought a heavy hand crashing down on to the boy's head.

'What kind of piano teacher is that?' asked Elliot.

'That ain't just his teacher,' said Kimorin. 'That's his dad.'

'Then why does he hit him?'

'Sometimes parents think they're being kind when they ain't. See, he thinks if he hits our little friend, then he'll get better at piano. Course, he'd actually learn quicker if he wasn't so terrified of making a mistake.'

They watched the boy play for a while longer. He was soon drenched in sweat and quivering, his fingers slipping on the keys. Elliot was torn between wanting to watch the boy play and feeling a tremendous sadness when he did.

'All right,' said Kimorin eventually. 'Now let's go in and get you another ticket.'

'Into what?' asked Elliot, turning away from the scene in the dreary living room.

'Into the house, of course. What else would we go into?'

'We can't just go in!' said Elliot. 'That's someone else's house. We'll get arrested.'

'Don't worry about that,' said the dragon. 'We're dippin' in and out of the river tonight, remember?'

When Elliot still appeared unconvinced, Kimorin added, 'I have it on good authority that when we walk through that door, ten years will have passed.'

'But that's not possible,' said Elliot.

Kimorin let out a snort of laughter. 'I'm a dragon and he's Ludwig van Beethoven, but apparently it's impossible for a few years to pass in a second?'

Elliot turned back to look at the unhappy boy pounding the piano keys as if seeing him for the first time. 'He's Beethoven?' he whispered. 'As in *the* Beethoven? The composer, Beethoven?'

'No,' said Kimorin sarcastically. 'The tumble dryer, Beethoven.'

Elliot threw his arms up in protest. 'But—'

'No more questions!'

'But—'

'There's only so much you can ask about, Olio,' the dragon said. 'Most things you have to find out for yourself. What if you was to ask me how a hornpipe sounded, or what cola tastes like? I couldn't tell you the answers to neither of those questions; you're just goin' to have to see for yourself.'

Without even pausing to see whether Elliot was following, Kimorin barrelled through the door of the old house, leaving the boy standing alone in the street.

Elliot took one last look at the child who would later become one of the most admired composers of all time, then followed the dragon through the door.

5

*E*lliot stepped through the doorway, only to find himself standing at the back of a vast concert hall. The packed rows of seats rose up and away from a stage framed by heavy velvet curtains. The people in them were staring, entranced, at the man on the stage. Their eyes glazed over with wonder and their mouths turned up in peaceful smiles.

Although he'd grown a bit, the performer was easily recognisable as the boy they'd watched crying at the piano just a few moments before. He was dressed in a long black coat, the fabric hanging in bunches at his knees. A bright red scarf was draped loosely around his neck and shiny black boots hugged his skinny legs.

Elliot recognised the piece of music he was playing too. It was one he'd heard Grandma Ellen play a number of times. It was difficult – incredibly difficult.

Even looking at the sheet music had made Elliot's head hurt.

But Beethoven played like it was as easy as breathing, his head tipped back and his eyes closed. Not a note was out of place. His fingers seemed to know exactly where to go.

The music tugged Elliot mercilessly towards memories of his grandma. To try and block it out, he shouted nonsense inside his head. He thought-shouted *AH FOR NAH GRAH* and *BAH FAR LOG LOO*.

And it helped a little, or at least it gave him something to focus on, other than the rising swell of familiar music.

Kimorin was oblivious to Elliot's struggle and seemed rather to enjoy Beethoven's playing. His tail bounced around behind him in time to the jumpy piano. His lantern tinkled. He even shuffled his feet slightly as though he was about to break into a dance.

Eventually, after a period of time that could have been a few seconds, a few minutes or a few hours, the music came to a halt. Beethoven stood up from his stool and gave the audience a small bow. Elliot could see his hands trembling as he bent at the hip. The man looked relieved, as though he'd just finished doing something incredibly dangerous. Elliot felt relieved too.

'Come,' said Kimorin, taking hold of Elliot's hand and attempting to drag him forward.

'We can't go up on stage,' hissed Elliot, trying to pull his hand free from the dragon's grasp.

'No one can see us, Olio,' said the dragon. 'Ain't you noticed that yet? We're like ghosts, 'cept less scary.'

To prove it, the dragon unfolded his wings and performed a jig in front of a woman dressed in an extremely stiff-looking dress. The woman only blinked a couple of times before patting her curled, blonde hair. She could see nothing but Beethoven. Her eyes had the glassy look of someone who had travelled somewhere deep inside their own head. A few rows ahead, a young girl in a blue dress twisted in her seat and frowned at Kimorin. The dragon didn't seem to notice.

Up on stage, Beethoven sat back down at his piano stool, tucked himself under the piano and began to play again.

'He's playing the same song!' said Elliot. 'Can't you make him stop?'

'Oh, come here,' said Kimorin, taking Elliot by the

pocket and leading him to a spot in the middle of the stage. They stood just behind the open wing of the piano. Even the quiet, delicate opening of the piece was much louder from their new position. Elliot felt himself start to shake. He could see the music acting on his body like an earthquake.

'Look at these people,' said the dragon, gesturing out at the rows and rows of people sitting before them. 'What do they have in common?'

'I don't know.' Elliot squinted, trying to make out the faces in the audience. Only one person looked as though she wasn't lost in the music: the girl in the blue dress. She was now standing on her chair, staring directly at the boy and the dragon. 'Um, Kimorin?' said Elliot. 'I think that girl might be able to see us.'

'Focus, Olio. What do they have in common?'

Elliot tried to focus. He remembered the stiff dress and noticed that everyone was in a similar stuffy outfit. 'They're all dressed like they're from the olden times?'

'Correct,' said Kimorin. 'They're all long dead. Every single one of them died before the invention of the iPad or chocolate cheesecake.' The dragon shook his head. 'Poor brutes.'

Elliot swallowed. 'But we can see them,' he said.

'They're right there.'

'Right again,' said Kimorin. 'When they heard our little pal Ludwig playin', they climbed out of the river. They left the hours behind. For the duration of his sonata, these people were plucked out of time.' Kimorin looked out over the audience as though they were lost puppies.

'How come we can see them?'

Kimorin smiled. 'I told you, Olio. Right now, we're out of time too.'

Elliot swallowed. 'So, music can take people out of time?'

'Music can take people anywhere,' said Kimorin. 'But you knew that already. That's exactly why you ain't been listenin' to any. But it's a mistake, Olio. Sometimes, we need to climb out the river.' Kimorin cleared his throat. A tiny jet of blue flame burst from his nostrils as he coughed. 'Just give him a listen.'

At the piano, Beethoven played.

The music flowed from his head, through his hands, and out of the piano.

It grew louder and louder.

This time, no amount of *BAH FAR LOG LOO* or *AH FOR NAH GRAH* could block it out.

The music took him away.

It took him to one of the countless afternoons he'd spent with Grandma Ellen. They were sitting in the living room, her with her cello propped against her leg, him with his violin tucked under his chin. They went over the same two bars of music again and again, trying to file them smooth like pebbles on a riverbed.

Grandma Ellen would laugh and cheer when they finally played the passage correctly, and they would have Hobnobs with sweet tea in celebration.

And after that they'd play along with quizzes on the TV.

And none of that would ever happen again.

Ever.

Because Grandma Ellen was gone.

Not to the supermarket or to bed or to visit one of her friends, but to a place you never came back from. A place that no one knew anything about. A place that wasn't a place at all; it was the opposite of a place – it was nowhere.

'Stop it!' shouted Elliot to Beethoven, waving his arms frantically in the air. 'Stop playing! Stop right now!'

Still, the music played on. Beethoven was oblivious to the sad boy, swinging his arms about like an aircraft marshaller. Kimorin watched him with a mixture of amusement and pity on his long, scaly face.

'I said stop!' screamed Elliot, running to Beethoven and trying, uselessly, to take hold of the composer's wrists and pull them away from the keys. His hands were unable to grip anything. They passed through solid objects as though they were made of smoke.

Realising the composer wasn't about to listen, Elliot once more jammed his hands against his ears and slumped to the floor. He shut his eyes and let himself shout out loud. 'AH FOR NAH GRAH!' he yelled. 'BAH FAR LOG LOO! AH FOR BAH GRAH LOG LOO FAR NAH LAH!'

After a few moments, a claw gently tapped him on the shoulder. 'Um, Olio?' said Kimorin slowly. 'You know how earlier you were askin' what a Hush-Hush is?'

Elliot nodded, swiping a shiny trail of snot off his top lip. His throat felt scratchy with all the shouting.

'Well, that thing over there, that's a Hush-Hush.'

Elliot looked up.

Standing at the back of the hall was a huge mountain of black hair. It was about the size and shape of a tepee. The hair that covered it was as long and thick as the coat of a Labrador. The creature seemed to have no

eyes, no nose and no mouth. All it had were two large, fleshy ears, which twitched either side of its body like antennae. The ears seemed to be searching for something.

Elliot felt sure the creature hadn't come to listen to Beethoven.

He turned to Kimorin with terror. For the first time since meeting him, he wished that his dragon guardian was bigger. Ten times bigger, in fact. And he wished he had shown more of a talent for breathing fire.

'What do we do?' Elliot asked.

'We don't make any sudden movements,' whispered Kimorin. 'And we speak very, very quietly.'

'What does it want?' whispered Elliot.

But Kimorin was distracted. As he'd done earlier at the fountain, Kimorin started sniffing the air. 'Can you hear anythin'?' he asked Elliot. 'Anythin' apart from old Beethoven?'

A great, low roar came from the back of the hall.

The Hush-Hush had heard them. Somehow, its giant ears had picked out the sound of their voices from over the piano melody.

Kimorin yelped. He sounded less like a dragon and more like a mouse that had just had its tail trodden on.

'You gotta find another ticket if we're gettin' out!' he explained hurriedly. 'And you gotta find it now, or else that thing's gonna reach us.'

With long, heavy strides, the Hush-Hush began bounding down the aisle between the rows of enraptured audience members. None of them could see it as it passed, though a few seemed to wrinkle their noses as though catching a whiff of a bad smell. Elliot looked to see if the girl in the blue dress had noticed the monster, but her seat was empty.

Elliot strained to hear something – anything – that might help them. But all that he could make out was Beethoven's piano playing and the sound of his own heart thumping madly in his chest, like a pigeon trapped in an attic.

The image of his grandma still came to him with the music.

'About now would be good, Olio,' said Kimorin.

'I'm trying!' insisted Elliot.

But he couldn't hear anything. And the Hush-Hush was almost on them.

He closed his eyes tight and focused. He could just about make out something under the increasingly loud piano playing of Ludwig van Beethoven.

The four notes of his nan's song, tangled up in the old tune.

They were coming from the same place as the music was: inside the piano.

The Hush-Hush had reached the stage and was manoeuvring its lumbering body up the narrow set of steps that led on to the platform. Elliot could already smell it. The creature smelled like stale milk and damp clothes and compost. It was an ancient, ominous, terrifying smell. Something about the creature's presence made Elliot freeze. He found himself completely and utterly unable to move.

'Olio, go!' shouted Kimorin.

On stage, the Hush-Hush let loose another deep roar. It was so close that Elliot could feel its breath on his face.

He closed his eyes.

There was nothing he could do.

Suddenly, the girl in the blue dress came barrelling out of nowhere, holding a trumpet in one hand and a green teddy bear in the other. She was screaming so hard her face had turned red. The Hush-Hush turned away from Elliot and growled. The girl swung the trumpet and the teddy in front of her like they were two great swords.

'Come on over here, you great hairy lug!' she hollered.

Elliot stared in amazement.

The Hush-Hush shook its coat of dirty hair in anger.

'What are you waiting for?' the girl shouted. Elliot took a moment to realise she was talking to him. 'Run!'

Something in her voice jump-started Elliot's body. He dashed across the stage and thrust his head into the piano, where the volume felt as though it was going to make his ears explode. A flash of white caught his eyes. Something was being tossed around by the wooden hammers of the instrument as they bounced off the strings.

With a flick of its paw, the Hush-Hush knocked the girl in the blue dress to the ground. It switched its attention back to Elliot and followed him to the piano.

Elliot reached further in, straining to catch the fluttering shred of paper.

The dank smell of rot filled his nostrils.

He stretched, trying to ignore the piano hammers passing through his chest. In that moment, he had a horrible thought – what if his hand passed through the piece of paper like everything else?

Dry, matted hair brushed against the back of his neck.

'BAH FAR LOG LOO!' Elliot shouted, throwing his entire body into the instrument.

The Hush-Hush roared.

As soon as he managed to catch hold of the envelope, Elliot felt the piano open beneath him like a trapdoor.

He fell.

And fell.

And fell even further.

Until he landed with a surprisingly gentle thump back on the train platform in Bonn. It was a cool autumn evening. A group of birds were watching him curiously from atop the station clock. Shreds of cloud floated in a dusty pink sky.

A pair of giant hands hooked under Elliot's armpits,

lifted him to his feet and dusted him off.

'There you chaps are,' said the conductor, stepping back with a smile.

'Oh, we ain't there no more,' said Kimorin, who appeared at Elliot's side. 'We're here now.'

He was right. They were back at the station, standing in front of the giant conductor and *The Night Train*. As before, the shadows of people cheerfully toasting and laughing and playing games shifted in the glowing windows. Elliot felt strangely reassured by the presence of the train. It wasn't home but it was a way of moving very quickly away from whatever that giant mountain of hair had been.

'Do you have a ticket for the next leg of your journey?' asked the conductor.

Elliot held out the crumpled envelope he'd managed to catch in Beethoven's piano. The conductor carefully prised it open, slid out the ticket and lifted it to his eyes to read the ornate, tangled writing.

'Interesting, very interesting,' he muttered to himself, before handing the ticket back and sweeping his arm to one side. 'If you fellows would like to hop on board, we'll be leaving promptly.'

The train whistled.

Bewildered, sad and exhausted, Elliot climbed on to *The Night Train.*

6

Back in the comfort of 444F, Elliot pulled one of the woollen blankets down from the luggage rack, draped it over his head and curled up into a ball. This was a dream and he was going to get it over with. He was going to fall asleep, wake up back in his own bed and never listen to Beethoven again.

'Olio?' called Kimorin. 'That thing ain't turned you invisible, you know. I know you're under there.'

'Leave me alone,' said Elliot, pulling the blanket tight around him.

'You weren't scared, were you? That thing ain't gonna get to you, not with me as your officially appointed guardian and protector.'

'It was that girl who saved me, not you.'

'Let's say it was a joint effort,' said Kimorin.

'I've called the police,' said Elliot. 'They said they're

going to come and arrest you for kidnapping me and they're going to put you in jail.'

The edge of the blanket lifted, revealing Kimorin's scaly face and giant, soft eyes. 'Police don't arrest dragons, Olio. Even you should know that.' They both stared at each other for a moment. Elliot, with his juddering bottom lip stuck out in anger. Kimorin, with his best attempt at a smile, which looked slightly more like a threat thanks to his teeth. 'Room for one more?' the dragon asked.

'No,' said Elliot. 'Not until you tell me what that thing was.'

'It was a Hush-Hush, like I told you.' Kimorin shuffled in beside Elliot. 'And a Hush-Hush is a big, sad, old creature without a heart. They live way out over the open ocean, but they come over here when they're huntin'.'

'What do they hunt?' asked Elliot.

'That's a good question,' said Kimorin, leaning closer to Elliot. 'You ain't gonna like what they hunt.' The dragon paused for dramatic effect, his smoky breath making Elliot's eyes water. 'What they hunt, Olio, is that thing that helps you 'ppreciate music.'

Elliot clapped his hands over his ears in terror.

Kimorin chuckled. 'Not your ears, you dollop. Your Spark!'

'What's that?' Elliot asked, lowering his hands.

'Your Spark is like . . . your inner ears.'

'What are inner ears?'

Kimorin pointed to his head. 'They're that special thing inside you that lets you feel when you hear music. It's the thing that turns a song from a few random old sounds into an emotion.'

Elliot couldn't help imagining that giant, creepy pile of hair from the back of the concert hall reaching in through his normal ears, and rooting around in search of a smaller, more delicate pair, made of glass.

'They can really take that away?' he asked, his voice barely above a whisper.

'They can and they do,' said Kimorin. 'It goes like this: most of you human persons lose your Spark after you've been on earth for around eighteen human years. After that, you only listen to music that you heard from before you lost it. You'll go your whole lives listenin' to the songs you heard as youngsters. Course you can hear other music, but it's not the same . . . it don't make you feel nothin'. It's a rare thing that you human persons can keep a hold of your Spark for longer than eighteen years.'

Elliot thought for a moment.

'I think my grandma kept it,' he said.

'I think she did too, Olio.'

A glum look spread over Elliot's face. 'But I don't want a Spark any more,' he said.

'And why would that be?'

'I don't want to talk about it,' said Elliot. 'It's private. I don't talk about private things with strangers.'

'I ain't a stranger, I'm a dragon.'

'You're a dragon I don't know.'

'We got plenty of time for gettin' to know each other,' said Kimorin. 'You ain't going home yet.'

'But I got another ticket!' said Elliot, throwing the blanket off in frustration.

Kimorin chuckled. 'So you did. Now why don't you take a look at what that ticket says?'

Elliot pulled open the envelope and slid out the ticket within. Written in the same style as the first one, it read:

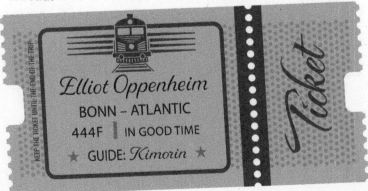

KEEP THE TICKET UNTIL THE END OF THE TRIP

Elliot Oppenheim

BONN – ATLANTIC

444F | IN GOOD TIME

★ GUIDE: *Kimorin* ★

Ticket

'Well?' said Kimorin. 'Does it say "home" on it?'

Elliot felt his bottom lip start to quiver. 'No,' he said, tossing the ticket to the floor.

'Then what does it say?' Kimorin bounced impatiently on his back legs like a child waiting to tear open Christmas presents. 'Where are we off to next, Olio? Don't keep me in suspense over here – I ain't one for surprises.'

'You said if I got another one, I could go home,' Elliot insisted. 'You lied to me. You're a liar!'

Kimorin shook his head. 'I ain't a liar and I never said you could go home. I said you could go somewhere. And we're movin', so you can't say we ain't going somewhere.' The dragon blinked at the boy, tilting his head slightly as though he was looking at a complicated puzzle. 'Don't you think your grandma left you these tickets for a reason, Olio?'

'Grandma Ellen left the tickets?' asked Elliot. Somehow, the thought hadn't occurred to him. He hadn't really had any time to wonder where the ticket had come from. Now that he did, it felt obvious. Who else would leave him a ticket that led him to Beethoven?

'Well, it weren't the King of Carrot Flowers,' said Kimorin.

'Who's the King of Carrot Flowers?' asked Elliot. Suddenly, all of the other questions inside him bubbled up at once too, until he felt like he might burst. 'And who are you? And who was that girl who saved me? And what exactly is going on? And why—'

Before Elliot could finish, the engine came to a juddering halt. Instead of telling Elliot off for all the questions, Kimorin began to sniff the air, his eyes widening.

Elliot climbed on to the seat and kneeled with his face to the glass, taking in their new surroundings.

He gasped.

All of a sudden, the carriage began to rock back and forth like a fairground ride. The lamp on the table slid towards Elliot then towards Kimorin then back again. Blankets tumbled out of the luggage racks. The sound of other passengers cheering and whooping hummed through the walls. Further down the carriage, something smashed with a loud tinkle.

'No!' said Kimorin, panic spreading across his face. 'No, no, no.'

'What's the matter?' asked Elliot, tearing his eyes away from the scene before him.

'I think I'm gonna throw up,' said the little dragon.

He managed to get as far as the door before letting loose a pale stream of magma, scorching the red carpet.

Elliot tried not to look. The sickly sweet smell of burnt sugar coming from the dragon puke was starting to make him feel sick too.

They were floating on an ocean. Dark waves capped with frothing white rose and fell around them, with the sound of someone searching for the right radio station. Above everything, a silver moon perched in the sky, its white light torn up into scraps by the foaming water.

With no sky and no land as boundaries, it seemed like they were amongst an endless darkness, stretching for ever in all directions.

7

As they disembarked the train, Kimorin's face had a slightly green tinge to it. He was carrying a copper bucket he'd borrowed from the train's toilet and looking about as glum as a student who'd just been called to the headmaster's office. The light in his lantern had turned a faint violet colour and his tail dragged along the ground behind him like a broken piece of luggage.

The conductor chuckled to himself when he saw the poorly dragon.

'He'll find his sea legs soon enough,' he promised Elliot.

'I ain't growin' no more legs,' muttered Kimorin.

The station they emerged into appeared to be built on the edge of a great cliff. Elliot thought it might be the trick of the water beneath them, but it felt like

...vaying violently with the motion of the
...gh he didn't feel as bad as his dragon
...ot's stomach felt restless, especially when
...ared to take a peek over the side. He immediately
regretted it.

Only a few narrow strips of rusted metal kept them
from tumbling into the churning water. Elliot made
sure to stay as far back from the edge as possible.
Kimorin, who was keeping his own eyes firmly on the
bottom of his bucket, didn't seem particularly bothered
about falling in. His wings had reached around to
cover his queasy face like they were trying to give him
some privacy.

'Where do we go?' Elliot asked, shuffling carefully
backwards as the train prepared to depart. 'I need to
find a ticket that actually takes me home this time.'

'Just keep movin',' mumbled Kimorin from behind
his wings.

The Night Train whistled and pulled away from the
platform.

A few steps out of the station, Elliot realised that
they weren't on the edge of a cliff at all. They were on
board a vast ship. A ship bigger than he'd even
considered possible. Below them, long rows of round

portholes glowed yellow. Over their heads, larger windows let out even more beams of light that illuminated four towering chimneys, all pumping grey twists of cloud into the dark sky. The air smelled of smoke and saltwater, and was alive with the hubbub of excited passengers.

Once again, Elliot caught snatches of music. There were the four notes of his grandma's song, but they'd been rearranged into a lively jig that dipped and soared in time to stamping feet.

'We're on a ship,' breathed Elliot. He couldn't believe it.

'I hate ships,' said Kimorin, yanking open the nearest door and throwing himself through it. The boy and the dragon found themselves in an atrium that reminded Elliot of a cathedral his nan had once taken him to. A wooden staircase wide enough to take a whole football team at once climbed up from the floor before splitting in two, each side leading to a long balcony that overlooked the magnificent hall. Bronze cherubs squatted on the bannisters.

The ceiling rose into a bulb of stained glass that cast delicate patterns on the white marble floor. Chandeliers made up of countless glittering fragments of glass, tied in webs by gold chain, hung overhead. It made Elliot feel as though he was standing in the atmosphere of another world. A bright, delicate world, where everyone was calm and smiling and pleased to see each other.

All around the lobby, passengers dressed in intricate dresses and tuxedos as black as the night stood chatting in groups. They held the stems of delicate glasses and nibbled on tiny, odd-looking food. The air crackled with excitement.

The only time he'd seen so many people dressed so smartly was at a wedding and he wasn't sure that people got married on ships.

The boy and the dragon made their way across the grand atrium. Realising Kimorin wasn't in much of a position to make a decision, Elliot took the lead. He chose a door at random and led them through it.

The corridor beyond was no less glitzy than the room they'd just left. Miniature chandeliers clung to the ceiling like jellyfish made of glass. The floor was covered by a carpet woven with intricate patterns of leaves and flowers. Square brass plaques beside the doors gave the numbers of the rooms behind them: 602, 604, 606.

'This ship is massive,' said Elliot.

'This ship smells like dragon puke,' muttered Kimorin.

Through a heavy door at the end of the corridor, opened for the woman in front of them by a waiter, they entered an auditorium. There, a man stood on stage before an audience of hundreds more elegantly dressed people. They were perched stiffly on heavy chairs, some deep in jolly conversations, while others stared expectantly up at the man as he cleared his throat.

'Can we sit down a second?' asked Kimorin. 'Dragons ain't meant to be on ships. Air or land only; we ain't hovercrafts.'

The man on stage definitely wasn't Beethoven and he didn't look like he was in any danger of playing music, so Elliot agreed, and they slipped into two empty seats at the back of the room.

A drawing of a ship that Elliot assumed was the one they were currently on hung behind the man on stage. From the drawing, it appeared to be even bigger than Elliot had imagined. Countless layers of cabins filled the space between the engines and the chimneys. The diagram featured arrows pointing out a gym, a swimming pool, a kennel, a squash court and a Parisian café.

The man was dressed differently to the other passengers. He wore a loose-fitting shirt with the sleeves rolled up, a pair of scuffed old shoes and a red rag tied around his wrist. His hair was long and floppy and hung in lazy curls over his green eyes.

'Welcome!' he boomed, silencing the crowd. 'Ladies and gentlemen, this evening I would like to offer you a brief scientific introduction to the magnificent, impossible, ground-breaking vessel that you're currently travelling on.'

There was a smattering of applause. People raised their glasses.

The man went on to explain that the ship was the first of its kind, as the people all knew. Never before had anything like this ship been attempted by the human race. It was a pinnacle of human achievement. They should all feel incredibly grateful and proud to be able to participate in what was destined to become a true piece of global history.

'On behalf of the captain and crew,' said the man, 'I hope you will all continue to have a wonderful voyage on this, the largest ship ever to have roamed the oceans, and the first ship ever to have been built in such a way as to render it entirely unsinkable.'

At that last bit, Kimorin looked up and spluttered, almost dropping his bucket.

'Are you okay?' whispered Elliot. 'I'm sure it'll stop rocking soon.'

'Oh, no,' groaned Kimorin.

'What's wrong?' asked Elliot, confused. 'Are you going to puke again?'

'No, you great dollop!' said Kimorin. 'You only went and got us tickets on the *Titanic*.'

Elliot sat up in his seat and took another amazed look about him at the elegantly dressed audience. 'This is the *Titanic*?' he asked. Could it be true? he wondered. Were they really on the most famous ship to have ever existed?

'You don't gotta sound so excited,' said the dragon. 'You *do* know what happened to the *Titanic*, don't you? It famously sinks, Olio.'

'But we're not going to sink,' said Elliot, uncertainty creeping into his voice. 'We're outside of time, remember? That's what you said! We're not really here.'

'Oh, suddenly he's the expert on who and what is outside of time, when two seconds ago he was munchin' chocolate cats on his way home from school and ignorin' lasagne in bed.' Kimorin lifted one wing to reveal half of his pale face. 'Even if we're outside time, we need somethin' to stand on.'

'Are you saying we'll sink?'

'I'm sayin' I've never sunk before so how should I know?' His wings enfolded him again as he let out a loud groan. 'Olio, I really don't feel so good,' he mumbled, his voice somewhat muffled. 'I'm gonna stay here with my trusty bucket, and you're gonna have to go catch us another ticket.'

Elliot felt his hands turn clammy. 'You want me to go alone?'

'Alone or splattered in dragon puke,' said Kimorin. 'It's up to you, but I ain't gonna be much use like this.'

Elliot felt sorry for the little dragon. Once, on a car journey to Scotland with his nan, Elliot had drunk three hot chocolates at a motorway service station and spent the entire trip being sick into a plastic carrier bag. Somehow, a trip that lasted a few hours had felt like it had taken his entire life. He knew how bad it could feel.

'Should I go and find you some medicine?' he asked the dragon, remembering that he had survived the journey back from Scotland because Nan had given him some travel sickness tablets.

Kimorin laughed. 'It's very kind of you to offer to look for funny-tummy pills on the *Titanic* when it could start sinkin' any moment now, but I think I'd rather you just go find us a ticket, so we don't have to spend any longer than necessary on this fancy-pants ship.'

'But where do I even start?' asked Elliot. The ship was huge – the small scrap of paper could be anywhere.

'Just keep your ears open, mugglenut. You managed it last time.'

'And what if I see a Hush-Hush?' Elliot shuddered as he remembered the smell of the mountain of hair that had almost caught hold of him.

'Then you run, and you sing. Sing as loud as you can, Olio.'

Elliot nodded seriously. 'Do you think I should have a weapon?'

'Sure!' Kimorin lifted his face from the bucket, a smile playing around his mouth. 'What do you want? A sword? An axe? A machine gun?' Elliot stared confusedly at the little green dragon. 'I'm jokin', Olio. I ain't givin' you a weapon, you dollop – you'll only come back with your own arm chopped off. Now go on, before I chuck up my other lung.'

Reluctantly, Elliot sidled out of the auditorium and into the corridor.

He could remember learning about the *Titanic* in a history lesson at school. Mrs Lyons had given them the basic facts, then let them watch the film with Kate Winslet and Leonardo DiCaprio. At least a third of the class had cried. Elliot had too. It was a strange morning, and everyone had been unusually quiet that lunchtime. No one had played tag or slaps or football. They'd just stood around behind the language block, asking each other how it must have felt to fight for a place on a lifeboat, or be trapped in a tiny cabin as it filled up with water, knowing there was no way out.

Something snapped Elliot out of his thoughts and he looked around. The passengers had stopped chatting and drinking and there were a few distant screams. Soon, panic filled the air and passengers began racing past each other, pushing and shoving, screaming and shouting. Glasses were being tossed aside; food was being dropped on to the floor. The colour had drained from people's faces. They shrieked like hunted animals.

There was a great, creaking groan and the ship tilted. Elliot fell, landing flat on his belly. Frantically, he tried to grab the carpet with his hands but failed. He slid what felt like the entire length of the boat. The carpet burned painfully against the skin of his belly as his T-shirt rode up, and his screams joined the others. All around him, people called out to friends and relatives. But it was too late.

The *Titanic* was sinking.

$\mathcal{E}$lliot landed with a thump against a closed door. Knowing he was running out of time, he hauled himself to his feet just as the ship decided to tip again. He managed to seize hold of the door handle. The metal under his feet groaned like a giant, mythical creature, awakening after thousands of years spent in slumber.

Not wanting to stay trapped in the narrow corridor, Elliot wrenched open the door and staggered out on to the deck. It was packed – clearly all the passengers had had the same idea as Elliot. Everywhere he looked, people barged and jostled each other, vying for positions in the lifeboats that hung from the side of the ship. A number of people stood and shouted orders, trying to organise the passengers so that women and children could be given priority, but their voices struggled to rise over the swelling panic.

Small kids were passed forward over the heads of waiting people. Not knowing what was going on, the kids cried, reaching their tiny hands out back towards their parents. The passengers below them begged and pleaded for spots. Some offered money or made promises or threats. None of which did any good.

It was useless trying to keep order.

Fights broke out and died away.

Lifeboats were lowered on to the ocean.

Tears of panic rolled down people's faces, mixing with the seawater that was being whipped off the ocean by the rising wind.

Elliot heard someone to his left mutter that there weren't enough lifeboats on board to fit everyone. This whisper quickly passed through the crowd. People grew more desperate. They struggled more fiercely against each other, scrabbling for positions by the boats.

Standing amongst the pain and confusion, Elliot felt paralysed. There was nothing he could do. It was such a sad, hopeless situation. And he knew how it ended. The whole world did. Not all of the people around him would get to go home to their own houses, towns and friends. They wouldn't sleep in their own beds again or use their own toilets or eat their favourite foods. Most of them would end up like Grandma Ellen.

Gone.

Lost.

Dead.

How many of these frightened passengers had children and grandchildren at home that were soon going to get the news that Elliot had been given two weeks earlier? How many people were going to feel how he felt, how he was still feeling?

It was too painful to think about.

And then Elliot heard the music.

It wasn't a complicated, showy piece like Beethoven. This piece was simple but stirring. It was the kind of song that made the hairs on the back of your neck stand up, your eyes water and your heart race. It reminded Elliot of a hymn, or a battle cry, or that song every adult he knew seemed to sing on New Year's Eve.

The song was coming from somewhere further down the deck, past the crushing mass of people.

Elliot swallowed. He gritted his teeth, shook his head and started making his way towards it.

He had to keep moving.

He had to focus.

He had to find a ticket.

He gave up dodging around people. He ran directly through them instead. It felt like dashing through a cold shower. It wasn't pleasant but he was running so fast he barely noticed it.

In a small clearing on the deck, he found a band playing. There were eight of them: three violinists, three cellists, one bassist and one accordion player. At first glance, each musician looked oblivious to what was going on around them. But as Elliot grew closer, he could see the fear in their faces, beneath a determination to focus only on their playing, keeping perfect time with each other. When they reached the end of one song, they'd pause for a moment to smile and laugh with each other, before someone suggested what they might play next and they started up again. The band didn't play like they were surrounded by chaos. They played as though they were friends playing for friends on an autumn afternoon.

Elliot looked around. Though there were many people shrieking and wailing, there were other people who had stopped to take in the music. Some held each other's hands, some swayed, some stood rooted to the spot, their eyes closed. A few looked almost peaceful, as though the music had taken them somewhere safe.

Not knowing what else to do, Elliot closed his eyes too. As usual, the song started asking him questions. What was he doing here? What was he looking for? What did any of this have to do with Grandma Ellen?

BAH FAR LOG LOO, he shouted in his head.

But even among the deafening panic of the sinking ship, the song lifted him up and away. It took him to a memory from a summer some years ago. For a moment, the memory flashed like a firework in his mind, so vivid it was like a scene from a film.

Elliot, his mum and his nan were sitting together in the garden. It was a Sunday – the kind of floaty, sleepy Sunday that felt as though it might last for ever. Grandma Ellen had turned up that morning with newspapers, fresh orange juice and a bag of croissants studded with chocolate chips. They'd eaten outside, while the neighbours mowed their lawns and the radio played through the current top ten chart.

That afternoon, without any warning at all, a great black dog had burst through the hedge. It was giant – so big that at first Elliot thought it was a monster. But both his mum and his nan had looked at the dog like an old friend. First, Grandma Ellen had started to sing. Then his mum had joined in. They sang a tricky, sad folk song, about a dog who ran away from the mean farmer who kept her locked in a dark basement. In each verse, the dog encountered a different animal and was given a piece of advice. The sloth told her to slow down and enjoy things. The horse told her that helping others would make her happier than helping herself. And the magpie told her to always look for the silver lining in everything.

It wasn't a song Elliot had ever heard before. When they were done, the dog gave a single happy woof before padding back through the hedge to wherever it had come from. Elliot had asked what the song was.

'It's nothing, really,' his mum had said. 'Just something your grandpa used to sing.'

The musicians on the boat finished the piece they were playing, only to begin a new piece, and Elliot's heart felt as though it had turned itself inside out. He wanted to break something. He wanted to tear the instruments out of the hands of the musicians and toss them overboard into the rolling waves.

It just wasn't fair that people disappeared and left

you alone. And it was even less fair that you had to constantly be reminded of that by music being played everywhere you went. Didn't anyone realise that music forced you to remember things? It didn't give you a choice. Listening to certain songs was like watching a film of your own life, starring the people who would never play cello, buy hot chocolate or sing to dogs again.

Elliot opened his eyes and realised that a tall, beautiful woman in a long crinkly dress was standing next to him. A necklace studded with dazzling green jewels hung around her neck. She was dabbing at her eyes with a handkerchief. Elliot couldn't help but stare. There was something about her face that made Elliot think he'd seen it before. Could she be a celebrity?

'Hello, young man,' she said, noticing Elliot. 'Do you need help?'

'You can see me?' asked Elliot, taking a step back.

The woman smiled. 'I can, and do you know, you remind me very much of my own daughter.' Fresh tears ran out of her eyes. 'I do wish I was with her now. But at least I know that even when I'm not there, she's got someone who will take very good care of her.' This thought seemed to cheer the woman up slightly.

She smiled through her tears.

'I'm sorry,' said Elliot, who imagined he had a pretty good idea of how she felt.

'It's not your fault, is it? Now, how about we go and have a look for your parents?'

Elliot wasn't sure what to say to that.

Ticket, he remembered. He was supposed to be looking for a ticket. Not standing around thinking about how unhappy he was and talking to sad strangers with big necklaces. There was no time to waste.

Elliot looked back over at the band as they struck up another tune. This time, it was a tune that had his grandma's notes embedded within it:

Elliot breathed a sigh of relief. If the four notes were here, the ticket couldn't be too far behind.

The woman beside him burst into a fresh round of sobbing.

He spotted a flash of white, emerging from the body

of a violin. It was his ticket off the sinking ship! It had to be.

Caught by a gust of wind, the envelope fluttered a few metres up into the air.

It hung in the night for a second.

And then it fell, jagging like a moth as it flitted towards the water.

Elliot paused, staring at the empty space where the ticket had been.

He glanced over the edge at the choppy water beneath. His heart beat in his chest like a snare drum. If he waited any longer, the sea would swallow his ticket. And then what would happen? There's no way Kimorin would leave him here for ever, was there? And where would 'here' be, anyway, once the ship had sunk? Elliot wasn't sure he wanted to find out.

Taking a deep breath, he launched himself over the side of the boat.

9

The water was freezing cold. It knocked Elliot's breath out of his chest. He tried to call out but there was no voice left inside him. All that came out was a faint wheezing, like a car that wouldn't start.

Elliot could swim, or at least he could normally swim. But in the icy, churning waters of the Atlantic Ocean, his arms and legs flailed uselessly with panic. The cold stung his bones and, no matter how hard he tried, he couldn't seem to take control of his own body. His limbs wouldn't listen to his head. His lungs were on fire. His skin was turning numb.

The nearest lifeboat was a dark speck in the distance. Even if they could have heard him, they wouldn't have come to his rescue. The lifeboats were already filled to overflowing, and there were still countless passengers aboard the sinking ship.

As the water crashed around him, Elliot realised he wasn't going to be able to keep himself afloat. He was fighting against the waves and the waves were winning. There was no way he could take on an entire ocean. Stars appeared and burst in his eyes.

Taking a deep breath, he started to sink. Elliot had never felt so alone. Not any of the times at school that no one would sit next to him or choose to be his partner during maths or pick him to be on their team in PE. All of those times, he knew that he still had someone waiting for him. Someone who was always on his side.

Panicked thoughts flashed through his head. If he drowned here . . . would he be eaten by fish?

Would he see Grandma Ellen?

Would Mum come looking for him? *Could* she come looking for him? Elliot still wasn't sure how *The Night Train* and the time travel really worked and he was growing dizzy with the pain of holding his breath.

And then he heard music, over the sound of the crashing waves and the screams of the passengers.

It was the band; they had started playing again. He realised with a start that he recognised the song they were playing. It was one they were often made to sing at school assemblies in the run-up to Christmas. Sitting in rows on the floor of the hall, they would sing along to lyrics projected on to the wall. And it was a song everyone liked for two reasons:

One, it was a fun, bouncy tune that was miles away from the boring, serious hymns that they spent most mornings slogging through.

And two, it meant that Christmas had almost come. The Christmas trees would go up, the mince pies would come out and lists of potential presents would be written. For Elliot, the best part of Christmas was that his nan would always take him to a concert. Even though they did this every Christmas, it still felt like a surprise because she'd never tell him beforehand what they were going to see. One year, it had been a metal band who wore masks and played between dazzling beams of fire. Another time, it had been Beethoven performed on a rack of wineglasses, all filled with different amounts of water.

He wondered what Christmas would be like now.

There would be no more concerts.

And no more after-concert cake, eaten while excitedly talking about the music they'd just heard.

Elliot felt his lower lip start to wobble.

He opened his eyes, expecting to see nothing but darkness.

Instead, two hands hauled him out of the cold water. He found himself squashed on a lifeboat beside the beautiful woman with the glittering necklace. She was shaking her head in disbelief. Water was streaming off him and his teeth chattered.

'Now why ever did you go and do that?' she asked.

'I'm sorry,' he said. 'I was looking for something and I couldn't find it and—'

The woman shook her head again. 'You do remind me of my Annabel ever so much. Always off doing something utterly reckless that apparently makes perfect sense to her.' The woman reached into her pocket. 'I wonder,' she said. 'Might this be what you were after?' She held out a shining white envelope.

'That's it!' said Elliot. 'Thank you!'

He reached forward, his dripping wet hand closing around the pristine envelope.

His eyes locked on to hers.

There was something connecting the two of them. Elliot couldn't put his finger on it and before he could say anything else, he blinked and found himself standing outside cabin 444F of *The Night Train*. Water poured from him as though he was a raincloud, turning the carpet beneath his feet a darker shade of red.

His hands and feet burned with pain at jumping from the cold water into the warm train carriage. Blood rushed back to his fingers and toes. His head pounded with shock. Elliot pushed his dripping fringe out of his eyes.

Standing beside him, a reassuring smile plastered across his face, was the giant conductor. His uniform was as immaculate as ever and he didn't seem in the slightest bit annoyed or surprised by the sudden appearance of a soaking wet boy on his train. He smiled the same warm smile he'd shown when Elliot had first met him.

'I'm already on *The Night Train*?' asked Elliot, confused.

'Indeed,' said the conductor. 'You were running a little late so I'm afraid we had to get the engine going. Best to make sure you get here in good time, though. If you're too late, we'll have no choice but to go on without you.' He raised a giant hand to his cap and tipped it. 'I presume you've managed to find yourself another ticket?'

Dazed, Elliot held out his hand and opened his

fingers to reveal a damp and crumpled envelope.

The conductor lifted it off his palm, shook off a few drops of water and peeled it open. Miraculously, the ticket within appeared to be unharmed. It was the exact same size and shape as the one Elliot had found under his pillow.

'Wonderful, wonderful.' The conductor smiled. As much as he felt it was rude not to, Elliot couldn't muster a smile to show him back. He felt completely drained, of energy and emotion and whatever else he'd once had inside him.

The conductor opened the door to 444F and signalled for Elliot to enter.

Inside, the little dragon was sitting on his seat, cradling a mug of tea. The colour had returned to his scaly cheeks and the light in his lantern was a rich, satisfied orange. He beamed when Elliot entered and lifted his cup in greeting.

'Where was our ticket, then?' the dragon asked. 'Wedged in a harpsichord? Hangin' off a xylophone?'

'It came out of a violin,' said Elliot, taking his seat.

Kimorin chuckled. 'And where was this violin?'

Elliot shrugged, reluctant to answer. 'There was this band playing on the deck, even while the ship was sinking. Loads of people were standing around listening. This woman with a big necklace saved me.'

Kimorin didn't look at all surprised that yet another person had been able to see and speak to Elliot. First the girl at Beethoven's performance, and now the woman on the *Titanic*.

'Sounds pretty excitin' to me, Olio. What did you think?'

'It made me think of Grandma Ellen,' Elliot admitted quietly. 'All music does.'

'And that's a bad thing?'

Elliot didn't know what to say. There was too much to put into words. Words were fine for describing apples or lamps or eye colour, but how could words sum up what he was feeling now? Of course it was a bad thing and of course it wasn't a bad thing. It was an impossible thing that hurt and made no sense at all.

'Olio, don't you think the music helped all those people? Can't you see how much it helped them to be carried to happier times? Those musicians gave them a gift – the gift of escape. Tha's a good deal more than the captain was able to give half of 'em.'

Elliot couldn't believe it had helped anyone at all.

'But they still died!' he exclaimed. 'The songs didn't save them.'

'Everyone dies, Olio,' said Kimorin softly. 'You and me and everyone we know. Sure, it makes it a little better if you're a hundred years old and have done everythin' you ever wanted to do, but this chapter don't go on for ever, not for anyone. The trick is just findin' ways to cram as many lives and feelin's and experiences into it as possible. That's how come we have music and stories and art and basketball.'

'You don't know anything,' said Elliot, sniffling. A fleck of snot had escaped his nose. He smeared it across his cheek, not caring how he looked.

'Ah, c'mon. It ain't that sad.' The dragon blinked as if reconsidering his words. 'All right, it is sad, and that's okay. Some things are sad, some things are happy. Like songs. What would a world with only happy songs be like?'

'Happy?' asked Elliot.

'Boring, Olio. And pointless. If you were happy all the time, it wouldn't feel like happiness no more.'

'Well, it would feel better than this,' whispered Elliot, folding his arms and slouching in his seat. A small puddle had formed around his feet. He shivered and pulled down one of the blankets from the overhead spaces. Since he'd last wrapped himself in one, someone had cleaned and refolded them. It smelled like a lawn that had just been mown.

The dragon didn't say anything more after that. They both sat in silence as the train thundered along on its tracks. Elliot dried slowly, staring out of the window at clusters of light tucked away into the dark folds of hills. They passed villages, hamlets and forests of trees so tall their silhouettes cut up the moon. It was still the deepest night. It didn't look like the morning was on its way.

'Olio?' asked Kimorin. 'Have you looked at the ticket yet?'

'No,' said Elliot defeatedly. 'Who cares what it says? It won't say "home" on it. It'll say something stupid, like "volcano" or "Honkenhanken" or "cheeseburger".'

Kimorin chuckled. 'Wouldn't you want to know if we were headed for Cheeseburger? Best to be prepared.'

Shrugging, Elliot yanked the ticket out of his pocket and threw it across the cabin to Kimorin. 'If you care so much, you read it,' he said.

Kimorin opened the envelope with a claw, slid out the ticket, and read: 'In Good Time, Elliot Oppenheim,

444F. Atlantic Ocean to Riga.' At that, Kimorin unfolded his wings and let out a squeal of joy. The ticket fluttered to the ground. 'We're goin' to Riga, Olio.'

'Why?' huffed Elliot. 'What horrible thing happened there?'

The dragon didn't understand. 'What do you mean?'

'All you did was took me to see Beethoven while he was being bullied by his dad and then the *Titanic* while it was sinking. If you're trying to make me feel better, it's not working. Why can't we see something nice?'

'You ain't seein' the point!' protested Kimorin. 'And you really think it's me choosin' where we go? I'm followin' you, Olio. They're your tickets. I'm just here to keep you motivated.'

'What about keeping me dry?'

'It ain't my fault you fell in the ocean.'

Elliot folded his arms. 'I didn't fall, I jumped.'

'Well, then, that definitely ain't my fault. You can't expect to jump into the ocean and not get wet.'

This was not something Elliot felt he could argue with. 'I'm going to nap now,' he said, lying on his side and pulling the blanket up to his chin. 'Please don't wake me up until everything is back to normal.'

'Ah, come on,' said Kimorin. The dragon nudged the boy with the tip of his wing. 'You ain't gonna nap.'

'You are not,' said Elliot.

'I never said I was,' replied the confused dragon.

'No, you said "ain't". You always say "ain't". But it's "are not" or "is not" or "was not", it's not "ain't".' Elliot fell quiet. Seeing the look on the dragon's face, he felt suddenly bad for having corrected his grammar. He knew how it felt to be told off for the way you spoke – it was like being told off for the way you sang 'Happy Birthday' or ate a muffin. It's not like you were trying to do anything wrong. 'Sorry,' he said. 'I didn't mean to be rude. Mum tells me off if I say "ain't". She says it's not speaking properly.'

Kimorin snorted. 'If you can understand me, then I'm speakin' properly enough. Besides, who's to say what's proper? You think you sound proper to a dragon? I ain't mentioned it before, Olio, but you sound a little like if Oliver Twist sat himself down on a hedgehog.'

Elliot felt his cheeks turn red. 'Mum says we should speak the queen's English.'

'What do you want to speak like a queen for?' asked the dragon. 'You ain't a queen, Olio. You're a violinist and an ignorer of lasagnes.'

'I don't play violin any more,' explained Elliot. 'I quit.'

The little dragon didn't look surprised, but he put on an expression that Elliot thought might be a dragon's version of disappointment. 'And did that help?' asked the dragon. 'Did it bring your nan back? Or is it just another thing to miss?'

Before Elliot could come up with an answer, the train had slowed to a crawl. The dark shadows of tall buildings fell in through the windows. Kimorin hopped excitedly up on to the seat to get a look through the window but Elliot stayed where he was, slouching in his seat with his arms crossed, and the blanket tucked around him.

The city that came into view was made up of towering concrete apartment blocks that stood pressed together like they were huddling close for warmth.

'Are we there?' Elliot asked. 'Riga?'

'I ain't sure,' replied Kimorin.

'Ain't you?' asked Elliot, smiling before he could stop himself.

'No.' Kimorin laughed. 'I ain't.'

The Night Train came to a final stop at a station that

looked somewhat worse for wear. The paint on the walls was peeling and flaking. The metal benches were rusted.

At least, thought Elliot, it was day again. Bright white sunlight flooded their cabin, momentarily blinding Elliot and he shuffled towards the window to get a proper look at the city.

This time, it wasn't the buildings that caught his attention. It was the people. Unlike Bonn, Riga was packed. But its inhabitants weren't milling about in crowds or rushing past each other with briefcases and coffee cups; they were standing in a single, long line, with their arms interlinked. The line ran along the centre of a main road, between apartment blocks, and on into the city. The people in the line stood with their chins out and their chests up.

'Those people look angry,' said Elliot.

'They sure do, Olio,' answered the dragon, sliding open the door of the cabin. 'Let's go and find out why.'

10

The conductor bowed as the boy and the dragon stepped off the train once again.

Together, they walked along the line of interlinked people. Even though he was sure no one could see him, Elliot felt nervous. There was something fierce about the people. They were like tigers, waiting for an excuse to pounce.

The line extended the length of the platform, through the train station and into the city. Between ornate, old-fashioned buildings with wooden roofs and white pillars, new apartment blocks had sprung up. These newer buildings were the colour of used bathwater. They may have looked new once, but dark stains had long since spread across their walls.

'Look,' said the dragon, pointing out a sign clasped in the hand of one of the people. 'They're protestin'.'

'What are they protesting about?' asked Elliot.

'Ah, now there's a question worth askin'. Ain't real easy to answer, though.' The dragon thought for a moment, stroking the long line of his jaw with a single claw. 'Have you ever heard of the Soviet Union, Olio?'

'Sort of,' said Elliot. He could remember his grandma mentioning it a couple of times. Whenever she did, she spoke about it as though it was a bad TV show that had finished long ago. Elliot decided that he'd rather find out what it actually was than pretend he already knew. 'But could you explain anyway?' he asked.

Kimorin scratched his head. 'Well,' he said. 'It was sort of like this big experiment to see whether people would be happy livin' in a place where everythin' was shared equally between everyone.'

'And they weren't?'

'They never really got a chance to find out. It's easy enough to share a birthday cake between ten people but try sharin' ten million birthday cakes between a hundred million people, every single day.' Kimorin came to a stop beside a rake-thin man holding a hand-painted wooden sign. 'The people in charge of handin' out the cake quite often end up takin' a bit more for themselves. And then they start marchin' into other places and demandin' to be in control of their cake too.'

The dragon nodded at the thin man and started walking again.

'But that sounds like a good idea,' said Elliot. 'Giving people equal amounts of stuff.'

'It ain't a bad idea,' said Kimorin. 'But only if you can be sure people get equal amounts.' The dragon paused. 'And if you can promise not to hurt other people in the name of sharin' cake.'

Elliot nodded. He understood, sort of. 'Where was the Soviet Union?'

'Well, all of Russia, plus a lot of other countries and half of Germany.'

'Half of Germany?' asked Elliot. 'How can it just be half?'

'That's a long story involvin' a long wall. Anyway, now we're in Riga. Which is the capital of—'

'Latvia,' finished Elliot.

The dragon looked impressed. 'Hey, that's pretty good. Where'd you pick that up, Olio?'

'I like geography. And my grandad was born in Latvia. My great-grandad too.' He glanced about at the strange city that had grown up around them. 'I didn't think it would look like this.' If he was honest, he wasn't sure what he'd imagined, but from what Grandma Ellen had told him about it, he'd pictured somewhere greener. Somewhere with trees and birds and fields filled with bored cows. The way she'd spoken about it had made it sound like the opposite of where they lived – somewhere you were more likely to bump into a wild animal than a parked car.

'Well then, there you go. Told you we were goin' places for a reason. It ain't just to see bad stuff happen.'

'I never met him,' said Olio. 'My great-grandad, I mean. Do you think he's one of these people?'

'If your grandma wants you to see it, then I'm guessin' it must have some kinda importance to her. Music, Olio, works as a kind of memory exchange. You remember some moment from your life, you try to trap the feelin' of it in a song, and then you play that song to other people. You find a way of sharin' your memories.'

'So this is one of my grandma's memories?' breathed Elliot.

'Or it's a memory she was given by someone else.'

'Who? My grandpa?'

The dragon looked annoyed. 'Olio, do we need to have another talk about questions? How am I s'posed to know who did and did not give your grandma memories? I'm a humble, garden variety dragon, here to keep you from fallin' into holes. I ain't the creator of the universe.'

Elliot thought about answering the question with another question but decided against it.

As they walked on, they passed fluttering flags and banners and placards, held proudly aloft. Some of the people chatted between themselves; others stood silently beneath their signs, staring squarely ahead like they were facing off with an invisible army. Chunks of dark bread and white cheese were plucked out of carrier bags, pulled apart and shared. Steaming flasks of coffee and mountain tea were passed around.

The chain continued on, no matter how far Elliot and the dragon walked.

Soon the buildings of the city shrank away and were replaced by smaller huts that flattened out as nature took over the ground. The sound of spluttering motors became the sound of twittering birds. The grey smog that clung to the city fell away – it felt to Elliot like taking off a pair of sunglasses. Faces brightened; the sky turned from grey to an endless blue.

Still, the chain of people went on.

It continued along the lane of a main road that ran between two walls of dense forest. The trees were spiky and almost identical. Mosquitoes floated lazily between their branches, searching for the juiciest people to feast on. The smell of sap and petrol hung in the air.

'How long does this go on for?' asked Elliot, whose feet were beginning to throb.

'That musta been a record,' said Kimorin. 'A solid ten minutes with no questions.' Elliot stared at the dragon, waiting for an answer. Kimorin sighed. 'It's about six hundred kilometres long,' he said. 'If I ain't mistaken, that's a fair bit longer than your entire country. There's somethin' like two million people holdin' on to each other right now.'

'Do we have to walk the whole way?' asked Elliot.

Instead of giving him an answer, Kimorin chuckled. 'Unless you sprouted a pair of wings since we was on the *Titanic*, then yes, I s'pose we do.' The dragon watched as the boy looked him up and down, had an idea, and opened his mouth to speak. He was quickly interrupted. 'Don't even think about askin'. I ain't a fairy-tale dragon – I don't give rides. You want to fly, you get on a plane. You don't jump on poor Kimorin like he's a seaside donkey.'

Elliot snapped his mouth shut.

A few moments later, the people started to sing in a language he didn't recognise.

Their voices surrounded him, music coming at him from every direction. He felt it take hold of his insides. It was inescapable. Birds left the trees and soared into the sky.

'What are they singing about?' Elliot asked.

'Listen to it,' said the dragon. 'What do you think they're singin' about?' Elliot opened his mouth to tell the dragon he couldn't understand the words, but Kimorin cut him off. 'Course words are important, but only because of the feelin's they can pull out of us, and notes are just as good at pullin' out feelin's as words are.'

For the first time, Elliot tried to let the music in. He tried not to fill his head with *BAH FAR LOG LOO* or *AH FOR NAH GRAH*. The sooner he let it in, he was realising, the sooner he'd find the ticket and get back to his own bed.

It was an unfamiliar song that didn't contain a

single English word. That didn't mean the music didn't take him places. As easily as any other song they'd heard, it caught hold of his hand and led him through memories.

His nan bursting into tears when a wonky old mug shattered on the kitchen floor.

His mum taking him to the little village she'd lived in as a child. Pointing out the pond she'd fallen into when she'd been his age. Telling him she was sorry that she had to work so much, that she was trying to arrange things so she could spend more time with him.

The three of them – Elliot, Mum and Nan, holding hot chocolates while fireworks burst apart in an autumn sky.

In the last memory to arise, Elliot tiptoed downstairs in the middle of the night. He was much smaller in this one. So small that his memories weren't full memories yet, more like blurry photographs. He sat on the bottom of the stairs, listening as his mum and grandma spoke in the kitchen. Both of them talked through tears. Something was wrong. Something was very wrong. Grandpa – a man Elliot could only remember meeting a few times – had died. They didn't say how or why.

Elliot could just remember a sadness in his grandma's voice that he hadn't heard before. *What am I going to do?* she kept asking. And of course, his mum had no answer.

Elliot opened his eyes. He had the sudden feeling of being part of something much larger than himself. All these two million people were singing the same song, feeling their own feelings but connected by the melody that was lodged in each of their heads. He wondered how many of them were thinking about people that they missed too. How many different things could one song mean?

'Well,' asked the dragon. 'What are they singin' about?'

'It sounds like they miss something,' said Elliot. 'And they want it to come back.'

'There you go!' said Kimorin. 'Who needs words? Words schmords, as I almost never say.' The dragon chuckled at his own joke. 'I think what they're missin' is a little bit of freedom. This, Olio, is what will go on to be known as the Singin' Revolution. The people from these three countries came together to demand independence from their Soviet overlords and music was the thing that they used to voice their demands.

The weapon they could all stand behind and hold up. You can ignore words easy enough but try to ignore a tune.' The dragon gave Elliot a knowing glance. 'As you'll have found out, it ain't that easy. They have a way of gettin' into our heads and draggin' up things we'd sometimes rather forget.'

Elliot looked up and down the line of singing faces. The idea that two million people were singing at the same time was exhilarating. The music rising up around him felt like it had the power to move mountains.

The boy and the dragon carried on along the chain of people. They moved slowly, with Elliot now making sure to look into each face, hoping to see one that he recognised.

Some were small and rosy-cheeked.

Some were large and dented.

Some were long and glassy-eyed.

Some were round and shiny.

Their voices, too, were as different to each other as their faces. Some were piccolos; some were trombones. Some were clarinets; some were violins. And somehow, despite the chaos, all of the different voices came together into one booming melody that shook the ground as it filled the clear air.

Further along the chain, Elliot came to a sudden halt. He was staring up at a man who stood with his head tipped back and his eyes closed. The singing voice that flowed out of him was deep and gritty. He stood with his barrel-chest out, his hands clasped in front of him, and his eyes on the sky like he was waiting for something to burst into existence. Smudges of dirt highlighted the wrinkles creasing his forehead. He had the worn, weathered look of a person who spent more time outside than in.

'That's him!' Elliot told Kimorin. 'That's my great-grandpa. I've seen him in photographs.' Elliot pointed to a wonky thunderbolt that ran along the man's cheek. 'Nan always said he got that scar by rescuing his best friend from wild dogs.'

'He's big, ain't he?' said the dragon.

'Do you think he's got the ticket?' Elliot asked. 'Should we ask? Or, I don't know, look in his pockets?'

As though he could hear Elliot, the man's eyelids flickered open. His eyes were a murky green, the colour of water in a birdbath. Unlike the passengers on the *Titanic* or the audience at the Viennese concert, the man's gaze didn't bounce off Elliot. Just like the little girl at the concert and the woman on the *Titanic*, his great-grandad's eyes fixed on the boy as he kept singing.

Elliot shuffled to one side and the man's gaze followed.

The song came to an end and the people cheered.

All of a sudden, the world felt too quiet.

'There ya are,' the man said, reaching forward with a heavy, thick-skinned hand, and resting it on Elliot's shoulder.

'You can see me?' asked Elliot.

'Today,' said the man, crouching slightly, 'I can see the entire world, and the entire world can see us. Let's not forget this. We are standing in the midst of history. People from every corner of the globe will come to know the songs we sang this afternoon.'

He crouched, picked Elliot up and threw him over his shoulder. The panicked boy called out to his dragon guardian. Kimorin only shrugged at Elliot.

'Help!' Elliot shouted. 'Get me down! I'm being kidnapped!'

'He ain't kidnappin' you, Olio, he's your grandpa. You gotta stop sayin' that everyone's kidnappin' you. Didn't you ever hear of the boy who cried wolf?'

'Not grandpa, great-grandpa,' corrected Elliot.

'And fine, maybe it isn't kidnapping exactly, but I don't know where he's taking me and I don't appreciate being carried like a PE kit!'

Elliot thrashed madly on his great-grandpa's shoulder like a fish washed up on the beach. A thick arm, soft with silver hair, clamped down on his back. The man carrying him smelled of sawdust and dill.

'Ah, quiet down,' his great-grandpa told him. 'I already got a headache. Let's just get ourselves home and make something to eat, shall we?'

'Put me down!' barked Elliot.

'I'm not putting you down,' the man said. 'I put you down, you'll disappear again. And I can't spend the whole night looking for you. We've got things to do.'

'I'm not your son!'

'Is that right?' the man said boredly.

It wasn't long before Elliot grew tired of struggling and flopped over his great-grandpa's shoulder. He hung with his face upside down against the old man's coarse shirt. Dirt, gravel and trampled leaves flashed past his eyes, making Elliot feel a little dizzy.

Kimorin, who followed along behind the two of them, was chuckling to himself at the turn of events. He didn't seem in the slightest bit worried about what was going on.

'Hey, he really thinks you're his son, Olio. You must look a little like your grandad.'

Elliot couldn't imagine that he looked anything like the white-haired man he'd met a couple of times when he'd been younger. That man had been so old and so big and so intimidating that imagining him as a kid was impossible.

Elliot had a thought. 'If he thinks I'm Grandad, then what does he think you are?'

Kimorin rolled his eyes. 'Olio, I'm pretty sure he ain't seen me. If he'd spotted a dragon hangin' around with his ten-year-old son, don't you think he might have mentioned somethin'?'

'But what should I do?'

'Enjoy the ride, Olio. That's all you can do.' Elliot thought he heard the dragon mumble something about being exhausted and wishing someone would sweep *him* off his paws for a change.

The man took great crashing strides down the road that led further and further away from the city. Unable to keep up on foot, Kimorin dashed up the side of a tree, leaped off and soared into the air.

It was the first time Elliot had seen him fly. From

below, the dragon was the shape of a kite. His wingspan was far wider than he was tall. The underside of his wings glittered as though they were stitched with golden thread. Kimorin looked like he belonged in the air.

The sky above the dragon warmed from blue to a pale orange.

Without warning, the man turned off the main road. Elliot cried out in surprise and his great-grandpa told him to quiet down. The old man carried the boy deep into the dark of the forest. High in the sky, Kimorin hadn't even noticed.

11

The trees were so closely packed together that barely any sunlight managed to find a way through. It was dark and cool in the forest. Woodlice nibbled on fallen trunks and brown leaves rotted to mulch under the knobbly arches of roots.

Elliot had no idea whether the dragon was still following them. The thought that he was now alone in a strange country with a strange man terrified him. He wasn't really alone, of course, but even though the man was a kind of relative, he was still a complete stranger to Elliot.

After what felt like hours, they came to a stop in front of a small wooden house built in a clearing. Logs had been chopped and stacked against the front wall. Two small windows cast a faint light across the forest floor. A wonkily built stone chimney released a thin trickle of smoke into the air.

The house reminded Elliot of the huts that children stumbled on to in fairy tales. It was the kind of house that looked cosy and inviting at first but turned out to be home to a witch who, for some reason, preferred eating boys and girls to chocolate muffins or chicken nuggets.

If his great-grandpa noticed Elliot's fear, he didn't say anything. He let Elliot down and marched directly into the hut, leaving the door open behind him.

Elliot told himself that the man was his family and that there was absolutely nothing to be worried about. He was outside of time, after all, and you couldn't eat someone who was outside of time.

Could you?

Elliot swallowed before following his great-grandpa into the house.

The inside of the hut consisted of a single room. It was difficult to believe that Elliot's grandpa and his great-grandpa both lived there. The last few rubies of a fire glistened in a soot-blackened hearth. Chains of wild garlic and dry scraps of meat hung from the ceiling on hooks. Two long benches were draped with scratchy blankets. This, Elliot realised, must be where the two of them slept. He hoped he wasn't going to have to sleep there too. Sleeping anywhere other than his bed at home or the sofa at his nan's house was virtually impossible for Elliot. On the few times he'd slept somewhere else, he'd had nightmares so terrifying that he woke up dripping with sweat.

Looking around at the cramped room, Elliot wondered for the first time where his great-grandma was. Surely his grandpa had a mum? But there didn't seem to be any signs of a third person and Grandma Ellen had never shown him any pictures of a great-grandma. Was she dead too? he wondered. Had she disappeared from his great-grandpa's life like Nan had from his and Mum's lives?

Elliot was knocked out of his thoughts by a potato bouncing off his chest.

'You peel, I chop,' the man told Elliot. 'Stop standing there like an empty pot.'

Not wanting to upset his ancestor, Elliot got to work. He knew how to peel vegetables. His mum had always said that learning to cook a few simple things was as important as learning to tie your shoelaces, write your own name or do your seven times table. It was helpful for him to learn so that he could put together dinner on the nights she was away for work and Grandma Ellen was around to help cook.

As Elliot peeled the skins off a handful of knobbly potatoes, the old man filled a pot with water. He dropped to his knees by the fireplace and gently coaxed the fire back to life with his breath and a few big splinters of wood. Once the pot was boiling over the fire, the man tossed in the hunks of potato. He added a fistful of dried meat, plucked from one of the roof beams, and stirred in pinches of salt and pepper.

Next, his great-grandpa went to one of the sleeping-benches and slid a battered old violin case out from underneath it. Elliot held his breath. The man carefully lifted the lid of the case and the sight of the instrument made Elliot's heart skip a beat.

It was his violin.

The violin that was currently gathering dust under his bed.

The violin that Grandma Ellen had given him on his tenth birthday.

She'd told him that it had been his grandad's and he'd have to take good care of it. If he was honest, he'd been hoping for a new one. He knew they didn't really have the money, but he couldn't help but feel like a new violin would sound much better than the dusty old antique that his grandma had given him. Of course, he hadn't said that at the time. He'd tried his best to look excited and grateful. He could see how much it meant to her and how much she wanted it to mean to him.

In the man's hands, the wood of the violin looked deeper and richer than Elliot remembered. It was polished to a warm, coppery shine. The strings glowed as though they were charged with electricity. The bow that his great-grandpa produced was perfectly kept, each strand of horse mane in its rightful place. Elliot thought of his own bow. It looked like a hairbrush that belonged to a dog.

'It's pretty,' whispered Elliot.

'That it is,' said the man. 'But it's not a painting. A violin's for playing, not for looking at. What'll it be tonight?'

Elliot still had no desire to play the instrument himself, but seeing it being handled so tenderly by his great-grandpa just made him feel guilty. Guilty that the instrument was gathering dust under his bed, guilty that he'd treated it so carelessly, and guilty that he'd decided never to touch it ever again.

The man sat down on a three-legged stool. He

tucked the violin under his chin, closed his eyes for a moment and nodded to himself. Elliot sat down too. As he did, he glimpsed a photograph standing on the windowsill. It was a crinkled, old-looking photograph, of a young man with a thick moustache. The man had big, blue, very familiar eyes.

'Sorry,' Elliot said. 'But who's in that photo?'

The man's eyes flicked open and he lowered the violin. He looked sadly at the old picture on the windowsill.

'My son,' said his great-grandpa. 'He's already gone over to England, wanting to start a new life. Can't say I blame him, but can't say I don't miss him either. It's a long old way. He sends letters, of course. Pictures of him and the wife and kids. Even asks me to move out there. But I'm happy where I am. This is my home.'

Elliot smiled at him.

There was no doubt about it. This was his great-grandpa, the man he'd never had a chance to meet. And the son he was missing was Elliot's grandpa, who'd already come to England and met Grandma Ellen.

His great-grandpa closed his eyes once more and lifted the violin. When he started to play, it was a simple song. Just a handful of notes that danced round and round in a circle. The tune was somehow happy and sad at the same time. It reminded Elliot of the way he'd felt when he'd moved from primary school to junior school. He'd been sad to say goodbye to his coat peg and his form teacher and his quiet spot in the hedge at the edge of the field. But at the same time, he'd been so excited to move into Year Three that sometimes he felt his entire body hum like a radiator that had just been turned on.

All of a sudden, Elliot felt incredibly sleepy. He could feel the song trying to convince him to doze off. *It's okay*, the song was saying. *You don't have to worry any more. Relax, close your eyes, drift away*. It was like the song was a warm bed.

Round and round, the simple melody went.

Happy and sad and happy and sad.

Elliot's eyes grew heavy.

No, he told himself. There was no time for sleeping. He had to stay awake. He had to find the dragon, find the envelope and get home.

Besides, who knew what might happen if he fell asleep while he was outside of time? Maybe he'd never get back home. Or maybe one of the big, stinking

Hush-Hushes would catch him and steal his Spark.

The boy forced open his eyes.

Through the small windows of the cabin, Elliot could see the faces of deer peering curiously at the old man with the violin. They stood perfectly still, their eyes shining in the light and their ears standing on end. He wondered what the music made the deer feel. Did it make them think of their relatives too? Did it make them remember spring days and cool lakes and juicy berries? Did it make them think of anything at all?

That was when Elliot glimpsed the envelope.

There was no mistaking the shred of bright white among the dim colours of the forest. It was clasped in the mouth of a bright-eyed deer.

Quietly, Elliot got to his feet. He didn't know how to say goodbye to the old man who was his mother's father's father. It seemed rude to leave without saying anything but if he did, he knew the man would stop playing and the deer would get away.

'Thank you,' he mouthed instead.

Elliot carefully opened the door to the hut and rushed around to where the animals had gathered to watch his great-grandpa play.

As soon as they saw Elliot approaching, the deer

fled in all directions, disappearing into the trees. Elliot was careful to keep an eye on the one carrying the envelope. It had a line of black spots along the back of its pale coat and darted like a ballerina through the woods.

He chased the deer, the music still playing behind him. He ran and he ran. His already aching feet stung as they came down on sharp rocks and twisted roots. His eyes strained to keep the animal in sight.

'Wait!' he shouted, knowing that the deer was very unlikely to either understand him or want to follow any orders he gave. 'I won't hurt you!' he called out. 'I just need that envelope!'

The deer kept running.

Over mossy boulders.

Under fallen trees.

Across streams of gurgling water.

Elliot struggled to keep up. His clothes caught on outstretched branches and tore. His laces came undone. Thorns scratched at his hands.

'Kimorin!' he shouted desperately. 'Help! The envelope!'

The music was gone. Either his great-grandpa had stopped playing or Elliot had ventured so deep into the wood that the sound couldn't reach him any more. He wished, for the first time since Kimorin had led him through the wardrobe, that there was a tune playing. He wished that there was music to give him courage and drive him forward. He wished that there was music to keep him company in the lonely gloom of the forest.

Elliot became aware of a smell. It was an ancient, rotten smell that knocked every other scent out of the forest air. The smell felt like a terrible omen. It sent a shiver of fear along Elliot's spine. The hairs on the back of his neck stood on end. Desperately, he tried to convince himself that the smell meant nothing. Perhaps it was old food or dirty water. It didn't necessarily mean . . .

He could barely make out the swaying shadows of trees and distant shape of the deer.

'Please!' Elliot shouted. 'Wait!'

His foot snagged on something and Elliot fell hard, landing face-first in the mud. It filled his nostrils and clouded his eyes. Spluttering, Elliot struggled to his feet. He tried to wade out so that he wouldn't lose the deer. It was no use. The mud clung to his feet and refused to let go. The harder he struggled, the further up his legs it seemed to climb. The mud wanted to swallow him whole, sucking him into the dark depths of the earth.

'Kimorin!' Elliot screamed. 'Help!'

The smell grew stronger and the wind picked up.

From somewhere nearby came the sound of a tall tree hitting the forest floor with a muffled crash.

Where was the dragon? Elliot wondered. Where was the music? Where was Grandma Ellen? Where had everything gone and why? Why was he so alone?

From nowhere, something caught under Elliot's armpits, lifted him high into the air and dropped him on solid ground.

The boy crouched on his hands and knees as he caught his breath. He hugged himself and rolled over on to his back. His mouth tasted like soil and rain. His lungs felt ready to burst.

'Thank you,' gasped Elliot. 'Why did you take so long?'

He wiped dirt out of his eyes and blinked until the world came back into focus.

It wasn't Kimorin standing over him.

It was a Hush-Hush.

12

The Hush-Hush was as tall as a bus. Shaggy hair hung from it in dirty bunches, splattered with mud and tangled with dead vines and withered leaves. At either side of its head, sagging, wrinkled pink ears twitched, straining to pick out the sounds around them.

Elliot shoved his knuckles into his mouth, biting down to keep from screaming. If it couldn't hear him, he reasoned, then surely it wouldn't be able to catch him? It didn't have eyes, only ears. Horrible, giant ears.

He scuttled backwards, trying to put as much distance between him and the beast as he could without making a sound. After a few metres, he found himself backed up against a sheer wall of ice-cold rock. He frantically ran his hands over it, looking for handholds or footholds.

There was nothing.

The cliff was as cold and flat as a slab of marble.

Elliot held his breath.

He slumped to the floor, his back against the rock. *It will be fine*, he told himself. *The envelope will appear or someone will come to save me, like they did at Beethoven's concert and on the* Titanic.

But there was no gleaming piece of paper within his reach.

And no friendly stranger rushing to the rescue.

The deer was long gone.

The Hush-Hush crept closer.

Two claw-like hands emerged from between its curtains of matted hair. The skin stretched over them was the oily green colour of old chicken. They smelled like compost and rotting fish.

Realising he was cornered, Elliot let himself scream.

'Kimorin!' he bellowed, with every ounce of energy he had left in him. 'Kimorin, help!'

But the dragon was nowhere to be seen.

The ears of the Hush-Hush wriggled wildly at the sound of the boy's voice.

Elliot curled up into a ball. He covered his eyes with his arms and pressed his forehead into the ground.

Surely, he told himself, this couldn't be happening. Surely, it was a nightmare. None of it made any sense. It was too weird and too horrible, and he was sure that he would wake up soon.

But the smell only grew stronger. So strong that it felt like it was coming from the inside of Elliot's head. More than anything, it was the smell that told him this was no dream. It was too disgusting and vivid and there was no way he was imagining the sick feeling in the bottom of his stomach.

The Hush-Hush moved its grotesque hands towards Elliot's ears.

It let out a sound that Elliot could only describe as a laugh – a kind of horrible, deep, sad laugh, with no trace of joy in it at all. The laugh echoed off the trees, reverberating through the forest until it faded to nothing.

Elliot felt long nails dig into his skin. The world fell silent. Completely and utterly silent. No birds, no bugs, no music. Elliot couldn't even hear the panicked thumping of his own heart. For a moment, he realised there was no music in his head. No favourite songs to be remembered, no lyrics to be sung, no melodies to be hummed. It had all vanished. It made him feel vulnerable and lost and lonely. Without music, he was stranded. He was completely stuck in time.

He tried to call out, but he couldn't speak.

The creature tightened its grip on Elliot's ears.

He felt nothing. It was like his soul was being drained.

And then the entire forest lit up.

A blinding light tore through the darkness, leaving nothing behind.

Every shadow was banished at once. Every leaf on every branch of every tree became visible and the sounds of the forest came rushing back to Elliot in a wave.

The dragon had come.

Kimorin swooped in a jagged path between the trees, violent orange bursts of fire spewing from his open mouth. His eyes reflected the twisting spires of flame. His great wings fanned the flames into great waves that rose and fell all around the lumbering Spark-stealer.

A searing heat flowed over Elliot. His hair singed and his eyes burned. His damp, mucky clothes dried out instantly, turning to cardboard. He lashed out at the Hush-Hush with all his might. His balled-up fists glanced harmlessly off the giant creature as though they were made of cotton wool.

The Hush-Hush roared.

It let go of Elliot's ears and drew its arms back into its coat. Elliot flattened himself against the cliff while the creature turned to face the dragon, the filth of its hair illuminated by the creaking, crackling flames.

For a moment, the Hush-Hush paused and watched the fire, trying to decide what it ought to do. It was trapped. On one side stood the towering cliff. On the other, a wall of flame. And above them all, the dragon circled.

The creature roared once again. It was a confused, pained cry that made Elliot think of dogs on Bonfire Night. If it hadn't just tried to steal his Spark, Elliot might almost have felt sorry for it.

Deciding that it would rather face the fire than the creature who'd made it, the Hush-Hush blundered wildly through the wall of orange. Its dank coat sizzled in the heat. The soot and smoke chased its murky smell from the forest air.

Kimorin landed with a gentle thump next to Elliot. The dragon folded his wings away and wiped his mouth with the back of his claw as though he'd just eaten a messy meal.

'Listen,' he said. 'I don't normally go makin' fire in forests. Between loggers and global warmin', there won't be none left if we keep lightin' 'em up. But dragon-fire goes out pretty sharpish, so don't you go worryin' bout that.'

Elliot didn't say anything. He was shaking and hugging himself like he couldn't quite believe he was still there. The muggy stink of the Hush-Hush still hung around his head.

'Olio?' asked Kimorin, gently tapping Elliot's shoulder. 'You okay? You get the envelope?'

'No,' said Elliot.

'Ah, well,' said Kimorin. 'We'll find it easily enough with that Hush-Hush out of the way. How was your great-grandpa's, by the way? Seemed like a nice enough guy – little on the big side, but that ain't a crime.'

Elliot didn't answer.

'What's the matter, Olio?' asked Kimorin. 'It's gone now, ain't it? You're welcome, by the way. Breathin' fire ain't a piece of cake, you know. Feels like you've just puked up a vindaloo, which I wouldn't recommend. Found that out the hard way, back when we was stuck on that rust-bucket kitted out with more chandeliers than lifeboats.'

That was enough.

'You left me!' exclaimed Elliot, getting to his feet. 'You left me, again! You left me on my own and that thing almost got me! You said you'd look after me! What kind of guardian are you?'

Kimorin raised his open paws. 'Woah, woah, woah,' he said. 'I'm sorry, I couldn't keep up with old grandpa long-legs.' He pointed at his short, scaly legs. 'I only got these little dragon stumps, Olio.'

'But you didn't even try! I bet you just rushed off back to the train to stuff your face in the warm carriage, while I was all alone in the woods.'

'You weren't alone and I weren't stuffin' my face. I was lookin' for you.'

'I was with a stranger!'

'You were with family, Olio.'

'Who I didn't know! How would you like it if I left you alone with your mum's dad's dad! He's not even alive any more. You basically gave me to a skeleton!'

The little dragon gulped, almost as if he was afraid of the boy. 'All right, Olio, you don't need to shout.'

This immediately reminded Elliot of what Lewis had said to him back when he'd been hiding in the toilet at school. *You don't have to shout, you know. No wonder you don't have any friends.* Anger burst out of him like a rocket.

'Don't tell me not to shout – I'll shout if I want to! Why shouldn't I shout? I'm sorry if that's why I don't have any friends. Maybe I don't want any friends. Maybe I had all the friends I needed and then they disappeared and now nothing matters any more.'

'Things matter, Olio,' said Kimorin quietly.

Elliot threw his arms into the air. 'Like what? Like music? Silly sounds that do absolutely nothing? Who cares about songs when everyone dies?'

The dragon shook his head sadly. 'You're askin' questions again, Olio, but you ain't listenin' to the answers. Who cares about songs? How about every person we met tonight? Those people watchin' Beethoven play, those people on the *Titanic*, those two million people standin' in a chain because they want their homes back. Don't you think they care? Don't you think your grandma and her grandma and her grandma all did? Don't you think you do? People don't holler like that about things that mean nothin' to 'em.'

Elliot didn't want to listen to the dragon any more. He turned back to the sheer cliff face and focused all his attention on a tiny dent in the rock. *If I just keep staring at that one spot, he thought, then nothing else will happen.*

All around him, the fire was sputtering out, inviting darkness back to the forest. With it came a chill that lifted the hairs on Elliot's arms. It was the middle of the night, and his only way out was likely to be miles away by now. The deer had probably even eaten the envelope. Elliot felt hopeless and wondered if he should just return to his great-grandpa's house and sleep on one of the wooden benches.

Elliot felt something cold and wet press against the back of his hand. He looked down to see the deer with the line of dark spots nuzzling him. It had a sorry look about it, like a child that knew they'd done something wrong. A pair of wide, innocent yellow eyes stared up at the boy.

With a sigh of relief, Elliot retrieved the envelope from the deer's mouth and gave it a gentle pat on the head. He wiped a bubble of deer spit off the envelope with his sleeve. The deer bowed slightly and darted back into the depths of the forest, skirting around the last embers of dragon-flame. Somehow, none of Kimorin's fire had left behind any lasting damage.

Only a faint tinge of white-grey soot dusting the tops of the greenery was left to suggest that a few minutes earlier, the entire forest had been ablaze.

Elliot tore open the envelope as the wilderness around him disappeared and he found himself standing, once again, on a train platform in Riga. He slid out the ticket. He sighed and rolled his eyes, shoving the paper into his pocket.

'You gonna tell me where we're headed, Olio?' asked Kimorin. 'Or is it gonna be another surprise?'

'Bourton-on-the-Water,' said Elliot. 'Whatever that is. Happy?'

'Well, that don't sound so bad,' said Kimorin unconvincingly, as if he were remembering the last train stop that involved water.

'I don't want to talk to you any more,' said Elliot. 'And I don't want you to come to whatever Bourton-on-the-Water is. I can do it quicker by myself. I don't need a slow, pukey dragon following me about everywhere.'

The lantern at the end of Kimorin's tail dimmed until it almost went out. 'That ain't a very kind thing to say, Olio.'

Elliot felt a little bad, but he stuck out his chin

stubbornly and stared the dragon square in the face. 'It's also not very kind to take someone out of their bedroom when they're just minding their own business and put them on a train and then leave them alone in a forest with a monster.'

With that, Elliot stomped away from the little dragon guardian.

13

eeing the looks on their faces, the conductor of *The Night Train* didn't say a word to Kimorin or Elliot when they climbed aboard in silence and slouched in single file along the corridor.

Passing by other cabins, Elliot could just make out the muffled strum of music and he scowled. He wasn't in the mood to hear anything jolly, anything sad, or anything at all. Or at least he thought he wasn't, until he remembered the feeling of total emptiness he'd felt when the Hush-Hush had tried to take his Spark. That almost made him grateful for the joyful chaos of the train.

Almost.

Not long after they'd taken their seats in the cabin, the conductor reappeared, holding a small pile of clothes.

'I noticed your uniform has had rather a rough time

of it tonight,' he said. 'I believe you'll find these fit nicely, young chap.'

'Thanks,' muttered Elliot, accepting the perfectly folded pile of lavender-smelling clothes. He turned to the dragon, who looked at him hopefully. 'Could you give me some privacy?' Elliot asked.

'Right,' said Kimorin sadly. 'Sorry. I forget. Best thing about bein' a dragon: ain't no laundry.'

The little dragon hopped off his seat and followed the conductor out of cabin 444F.

Alone, Elliot climbed out of his muddy, shredded clothes and put on the ones the conductor had given him. The new outfit consisted of beige trousers with side pockets, a loose-fitting shirt, and a pair of polished leather boots. It was the kind of ensemble Elliot imagined explorers wearing to trek across deserts and shoulder paths through the jungle.

He had no idea how he was going to explain this change to his mum. She'd be furious that he'd destroyed another school uniform. Usually, she tried her best to patch and sew them back together, but if he came home with all his clothes missing, they'd have to buy an entire new set. Elliot knew that wouldn't be easy. It would probably mean emptying the old ice-cream tub that they used to collect spare change so that they could go to the cinema once a month.

The fresh clothes didn't do much to raise Elliot's spirits. Bourton-on-the-Water was next, wherever that was, but who knew how many other places would come after. How long would it be before he was back home? Kimorin either didn't know or didn't want to tell him. It was beginning to feel as though he would be riding *The Night Train* for ever.

He watched the woods cycle past the window. As the train thundered along, their leaves gradually changed from spiky needles of drab green to wide, bright leaves that glittered in the rising sun.

Elliot's attention was pulled away from the trees by an unexpected voice.

'Anyone home?'

The door to 444F had opened slightly and a face had appeared in the gap. It was a woman's face, framed with coppery hair and arranged in an apologetic smile. A pair of thick, caterpillar eyebrows sat over two beady green eyes. Her cheeks and the tip of her nose shone with cold.

'Sorry to intrude,' said the woman. She was dressed in mud-splattered camouflage gear and holding an umbrella that had been turned inside-out. 'But do you mind if I take a seat? Every other cabin is either taken or incredibly noisy.'

'No,' said Elliot, pointing at the free seats. 'There's room.'

Part of him hoped that if Kimorin looked in and saw the woman sitting there, he wouldn't come in. Just looking at the dragon made him furious. It was hard not to blame him for everything that had happened. He'd been the one to drag Elliot out of his warm bed and into the night, after all.

After tossing the umbrella into one of the overhead racks, the woman kicked off her shoes and peeled off her socks.

'So,' the woman said, making herself comfortable in the seat opposite Elliot's. 'What are you riding *The Night Train* for?'

Elliot didn't really know how to answer that. 'I found a ticket under my pillow,' he said simply. 'Then a dragon came to get me.'

The woman unwound a scarf from around her neck, folded it on her lap and stroked it like a cat. 'How lucky,' she said. 'It's a wonderful gift, a ticket to ride this old train, wherever it might take you.'

'Doesn't feel like it,' muttered Elliot.

'It doesn't?' she asked, her heavy eyebrows rising up into her wispy fringe.

'No,' said Elliot. 'Actually, it feels like the opposite. It feels completely pointless and sad and stupid.'

The woman looked shocked by this opinion. She'd obviously had a completely different experience to him. Maybe she'd been given a guardian who didn't abandon her or lie to her or take her on to ships just as they were about to sink. Maybe her guardian never puked. A small voice in his head told him off for being harsh. Kimorin couldn't control those things. But Elliot pushed that voice aside. From the look of the woman, though, her guardian hadn't managed to keep her very dry either.

'May I ask your name?' the woman said, after a few moments had passed.

'Elliot.'

'Elliot,' repeated the woman. 'I'm Amina, and I'd like to tell you a story, if that's okay.'

Not wanting to be rude, Elliot nodded.

The woman cleared her throat and started to talk. 'Many, many years ago, I lost my husband in a traffic accident.'

Elliot couldn't tell if he was supposed to tell her he was sorry. Ever since his nan had died, people had been telling him they were sorry, but sorry was a word that felt as helpful as 'cucumber' or 'bagpipes'. What good was 'sorry' supposed to do? Still, Elliot guessed it was the polite thing to say.

'I'm sorry,' he said.

'Aren't we all?' said the woman. Elliot wasn't quite sure what she meant by that, but he didn't ask. 'As you can imagine,' she continued, 'it was the worst day of my life. One moment he was there, the person I cared about more than anyone else in the world, and the next he was . . . gone. There didn't seem to be any reason. No one could explain to me why it had happened. To be honest, an explanation wouldn't have helped anything. It's not like it would have brought him back.'

Elliot bit his lip. He understood.

'With him gone, I moved in with my sister. I refused to go back to our house. I didn't want to be near anything that reminded me of him. I didn't want to think of him at all. It was too painful. So, I started avoiding anything that reminded me of him. I wouldn't play any of the board games we'd used to play, watch the films we'd used to watch, or listen to the music we'd used to listen to. I even moved out of the house we'd shared.'

The woman's nose started to run. She patted her pockets in search of a tissue but found nothing. Without thinking, Elliot slid a hand into his new trousers and discovered a handkerchief. He held it out to the woman, who accepted it with a smile and a grateful nod.

'Thank you,' she said, blowing her nose.

A moment later, she continued her story.

'Then, one day, I was reading in a coffee shop near her house. I popped to the bathroom and when I came back, there was an envelope tucked into the pages of my book. You may have guessed what that envelope contained.'

Elliot nodded. 'It was a ticket to ride this train.'

The woman leaned in close to Elliot as though she was about to tell him a secret. 'I won't tell you what I encountered during my first journey,' she said. 'There would be no point. We each follow our own routes on this train – that's the beauty of it. We could never understand the places that other people visit. But I will tell you this: on my journey I realised that there were parts of my husband in that house and in those films and in that music. All the time we'd spent enjoying them together meant they became places where I could go to be with him. It was through the things we'd shared that I could bring him close. So, I learned to cherish them, not to be afraid of them.'

The woman smiled, eyes shining. 'And do you know the amazing thing about music?'

Elliot shook his head.

'The amazing thing about music, about all sound, is that it's never-ending. The sound waves we all make just go on travelling endlessly into the universe. The music we make lives for ever.'

Elliot didn't know what to say. He felt bad for the woman, but he also didn't think she made much sense. He didn't feel closer to Grandma Ellen when he heard music; he felt further away. It was just a reminder that she wasn't there any more. She wasn't in her living room or the bathtub or waiting outside the school gates to tell him about a new recording of an old symphony she'd discovered in a record shop. She was nowhere. And that wasn't going to change.

'I need the toilet,' Elliot said, getting to his feet and dashing out of the cabin.

In the corridor, he found Kimorin, standing like a guilty child by the photographs of musicians. The lantern at the end of his tail was the colour of toothpaste. He looked smaller than Elliot remembered, and his wings hung loosely at his back as though they were tired.

Kimorin opened his mouth to speak.

Elliot shouldered his way past the dragon and started walking. Paying no attention to anything around him, he carried on down the train. Through carriage after carriage, he walked, throwing open the doors between them with such force that their hinges squeaked like frightened mice.

Where was he hoping to go? It wasn't like things would be any different at the other end of the train. But he hadn't wanted to sit still in that cabin, hearing how much music could mean to you after someone had died. He was happy the woman had found a way of missing her husband less but there was no way it was going to work for him. He was never going to miss Grandma Ellen less. He was never going to sit around listening to her music and watching her films and remembering that she used to be here but now she wasn't.

'Next stop, Bourton-on-the-Water,' called the voice of the conductor.

The train slowed to a halt.

Elliot did too.

He looked out of the window to his right.

It was late afternoon.

They were back in England. Green fields spread out around the train tracks, split into squares by lush hedges. The rosy pink of the sky suggested it was starting to put on its evening clothes. Elliot could make out the stone tower of a church, poking out from a cluster of cottages and into the clouds. A weathervane shaped like a deer spun like a merry-go-round on its spire.

14

The conductor gave Elliot a questioning look as the boy climbed off the train alone. Elliot didn't bother stopping to explain that, no, the dragon wasn't coming with him. And no, he didn't want to talk about it. The tickets were supposed to be for him, after all, not for Kimorin. What did it matter whether he took the dragon with him or not?

The train station was the smallest they'd stopped at yet. It was barely more than a raised platform at the edge of a field, with a low, wooden shelter casting a shadow over it. Yellowed timetables peeled off the flimsy walls. An old leather suitcase with rusted buckles lay forgotten under a bench.

Everything smelled of manure and pollen. It was the dusty, hazy kind of warm that settled in at the end of a blisteringly hot day. If Elliot had been at school, it would have been the sort of day he'd spend longing to be outside.

School.

Even the prospect of school felt comforting now. It was dull and long and filled with things he didn't want to do, but at least he always knew what would come next. No one at school ever sent him to random places without warning or tried to steal his Spark.

Looking down, Elliot noticed that the floor of the station was littered with ragged squares of paper. At first, he thought they were used train tickets, but a second look showed that all they had written on them were names. The names had been handwritten in the same spidery writing. Elliot wondered what they could be. They were nametags, he supposed. But for whom? And why had they been left on the ground?

The Night Train's whistle pierced the calm autumn afternoon. Elliot turned to face the almost-endless chain of carriages and the conductor waved to him. In the cabins, people played and spoke and sang and ate. No one else seemed to be getting off at this stop. Not even Kimorin, who Elliot had half-expected to bound out after him despite what he'd said back in the forest by Riga. Had he really meant it? Did he really want to carry on without the dragon?

The Night Train disappeared into the green hills of England. With it went the upset face of the little dragon, pressed to the window of carriage 444F. Elliot tried to keep his thoughts focused on the task at hand. He wasn't responsible for the dragon's feelings; the dragon was supposed to be the one looking after him. He shouldn't feel bad.

Anyway, what was he supposed to do now? Kimorin was gone and he had to find another ticket. There was no point adding something else to the list of things he already felt sad about.

Kicking at the papers that littered the floor, Elliot heard music.

It wasn't the simple tune that had played on the tape in his bedroom, but the tricksy piece they'd heard Beethoven perform back in Bonn. The same piece Grandma Ellen loved to play. A piece that Elliot knew he would never even come close to mastering.

Whoever was playing it now hadn't quite got the hang of it either. Far from the fluid playing of its composer, the person was tripping and stumbling over the melody in a way that made Elliot wince. Although a few passages came out naturally, there were long pauses and wrong notes added to every bar. This, together with the fact that it was being played on a slightly out-of-tune piano, made the piece sound almost sinister.

Elliot wondered whether the person had just started learning the tune or whether they'd chosen something that was too difficult for them. He knew that whenever he began to learn a tough piece, it always sounded unrecognisable at first. As his violin teacher had always said: practice isn't for sounding good, it's for getting good.

Elliot took a deep breath.

No *AH FOR NAH GRAH.*

No *BAH FAR LOG LOO.*

Not this time.

He walked out of the train station and into a village of winding streets and thatched cottages, with thick vines of ivy that crept over the windows. The only cars Elliot spotted were strange-looking, bubbly-shaped things, with long bonnets and giant headlights that sat over the wheels like bug eyes. Bicycles fitted with wicker baskets rested against splintered garden fences. A narrow stream ran through the centre of the village, its banks shored up with mossy stones. Ancient willows watched their own reflections in the water. Small, arched bridges built of rock linked one side to the other.

There was no one in the streets, but Elliot had got used to that. Not everyone was outside time in these places, he'd learned. Time moved on and didn't leave many people behind. Only those few who were lucky enough to be lost in music.

Elliot followed the melody up more cobbled streets and past wonky terraced houses built of yellow stone. A kind of determination grew in him as he went; he would find wherever it was coming from, he would find the next ticket, and he would find however many other tickets he needed to get home. He had no other choice. There was no way he was staying on that train for ever. And once he got off, he wouldn't get back on. He wouldn't be like Amina. He wouldn't look back, ever.

Elliot came to a stop outside a small church. Stained-glass windows cast dappled light on to the perfectly manicured lawn and a single oak tree stood guard over lines of well-kept graves.

Standing in the shadow of the impressive building was a much smaller, much more rundown construction, built of rickety-looking pieces of wood.

It looked like one of the huts that surrounded Elliot's school – huts they used for music lessons, club meetings and play rehearsals. It was always either much too cold or much too hot in the huts. Elliot dreaded having to venture out to the shabby little buildings.

But, by that point, he knew what he had to do. If he wanted an envelope, he had to follow the music.

And the music was coming from the hut.

Elliot marched through a wonky door, into a dark, low-ceilinged room. In the back corner, a girl stood alone at an upright piano. Like young Beethoven, she was too short to reach the keys properly, and so had built herself a platform from a set of encyclopaedias. She was squinting at wrinkled pages of sheet music. It was strange to think that the music she was stumbling her way through was music that had been written by that scared, young boy Elliot had encountered earlier that night. It made the idea of time itself, the way that one thing happened after another, feel almost unbelievable.

He waited patiently in the middle of the room, casting his eyes about for a glimpse of white. There was nothing yet. But perhaps it was too soon.

The girl finished playing.

She shook her head in frustration and stared at her hands angrily.

Elliot wondered whether she'd be able to see him, like the girl in the blue dress, the woman with the sparkling necklace and his great-grandpa back in Riga.

Wanting to find out, Elliot cleared his throat.

The girl swivelled around on her stack of old encyclopaedias.

'Hello,' she said, not sounding particularly frightened by the sudden appearance of a boy.

Elliot tried to force a smile. 'Hi,' he said. 'Can you see me?'

'Of course I can see you. Can you see me?'

'I can see you,' said Elliot. 'It would be a little strange if I couldn't, since I was the one who asked first.'

The girl smiled. 'Did you come to play piano too? I always wanted to play piano but there's no way we could ever have one at home, so it was nice to find one in this village. They're really expensive, you know. And they take up so much room. I suppose you could always sleep on it, or under it. I don't think I'd mind that at all.'

The girl spoke so quickly that Elliot almost struggled

to keep up. 'This village isn't your home?'

'Oh, no,' the girl said. 'My home is miles away. You have to go on a train if you want to get there and believe me, you don't want to go on that train. Not unless you've got a stomach made out of iron, which I don't. Mum says I have a stomach made out of melted ice cream and fig rolls. She said that if you unzipped me, you'd find a sweet shop.'

'So, you're on holiday?'

'Sort of,' the girl said, a look of sadness sinking into her face. 'But not really.'

'What do you mean?' Elliot asked.

The girl raised an eyebrow, looking at Elliot with curiosity. 'Don't you know? The bombs are falling on cities, so they sent all us children here to the countryside where we'll be safer. You must live here if you hadn't known about the evacuations?' Before Elliot could answer, she continued. 'It's okay, though, everyone says the war will be over soon. Then we'll get to go home again.'

In school, Elliot could remember learning about the evacuations that took place during the Second World War. Thousands and thousands of children had been sent away from their homes in cities to live with strangers in the countryside. It was a way of keeping them safe, he understood that, but he couldn't help thinking that living with people you didn't know might have been almost as terrifying as hearing bombs fall around you at night.

'You're an evacuee?' he said. Suddenly, the nametags on the floor of the station made sense. The kids had been forced to wear them on the train so they could be organised and brought off at the right stops. Once they'd been passed over to the people they'd be staying with, there was no need for them to wear the tags any more, and many of them must have ripped them off.

'I suppose I'm an evacuee,' said the girl. 'But I hope I won't be one for much longer, and I'm lots of other things too.' She was quiet for a moment, her brow furrowed. 'I do like being with the piano, but I also miss home terribly.'

'You're learning Beethoven,' Elliot said, attempting to distract her from her sadness. 'I recognise it. My nan plays it all the time.'

'Really? I actually learned it ages ago,' the girl said. 'But I didn't learn it on a normal piano. I learned it on a chalk piano. So now I have to learn it all over again.'

'What's a chalk piano?'

'It's when you draw a piano in chalk on the floor and play it on there.' She stuck out her chin as though daring Elliot to suggest that a 'chalk piano' wasn't a real thing at all. He didn't. He was too busy feeling impressed that she'd managed to learn to play such an incredibly difficult piece without ever touching an instrument.

'You can play like that and you've never even touched a real piano?'

'Well,' she said. 'I've been here two weeks now, but I've only been able to sneak off six times. I tell the Gopshurts that I'm going to help the vicar clean the church. They're the people I'm staying with. They're okay, but their house smells like mackerel and they make me give them foot rubs.'

'That's amazing,' said Elliot. 'You're really good.'

The girl looked pleased. 'Do you play piano too?' she asked.

'A little bit,' said Elliot. 'But mostly I play violin.'

'Ooh,' the girl said. 'I've always wanted to try playing violin. Do you have your own one? Do you practise every day? What's your favourite song to play? Can you show me?'

Elliot wasn't sure which of her questions to answer first. He wasn't sure how to answer them either. The idea that he was lucky to have an old violin under his bed had never really occurred to him. He supposed that if he'd had to learn by playing something he'd drawn on the floor, then he'd probably think he was lucky too.

'I don't have my violin with me,' said Elliot. 'Anyway, I don't play it any more.'

'Why not?'

'It's a long story,' said Elliot, who really wanted to talk about something different. 'You haven't seen an envelope, have you? A really white one?'

The girl shook her head.

Taking another look around the dingy hall, Elliot noticed a crumpled, greenish-looking teddy bear lying on the floor a few metres from the piano. He bent down to pick it up. As his hands closed around the toy, the girl let out a shriek.

'Don't touch him!' she shouted, reaching forward.

Elliot, who hadn't meant to cause any harm, immediately handed over the soft toy to the girl. As he did, he realised it wasn't a teddy at all. It was a small, plush dragon, made out of different shades of cloth.

Two glass beads formed the eyes. A shred of orange fabric lolled out of the mouth like a flame. Elliot was stunned. It almost looked like . . .

'Sorry,' said the girl, tucking the soft dragon safely under her arm. 'I didn't mean to snap, but I don't like it when other people touch him. He's very special to me. Sometimes, the girls from the farm up the road steal him and hide him and I have to spend hours looking through the barns to find him. I know he's not real, but I can't help feeling that he gets cold and lonely.'

'That's mean of them,' said Elliot.

The girl blew out her cheeks like a squirrel and nodded. 'Yes,' she said. 'It is. But if I come here, they can't find me. The vicar doesn't mind if I stay in here the whole day on my own. Well, alone except for Kimorin. But it's the Gopshurts who get cross.'

'That's really Kimorin?' asked Elliot, pointing at the slightly squashed dragon clamped in the girl's armpit.

The girl wrinkled her shiny forehead. 'How do you know Kimorin?' she asked suspiciously.

Elliot wasn't really sure how to respond. He knew telling her that they were friends would make it seem as though he was either very stupid or talking complete nonsense. Anyway, were they still friends? Had they ever been friends? Elliot found it hard to tell. He didn't have a lot of experience with friends. 'I think I might have seen him in a dream,' he said. 'Or I maybe I saw another version of him?'

'I'm not sure you did,' the girl said. 'My grandma gave him to me, and her grandma gave Kimorin to her. There are no others like him anywhere. Most dragons are fearsome, but not Kimorin. He's a friendly dragon. Friendly unless you're mean to me, in which case he can grow rather unfriendly.'

'Your grandma gave him to you?'

'Yes, and she's not here any more so I need him. Actually, I never got to meet her. But she gave Kimorin to my mum and then my mum gave him to me. She said he'll protect me, no matter where I go. Nothing can hurt me as long as I have Kimorin.'

Elliot felt a looming sense of dread. Everywhere he went and every person he spoke to seemed to have a sad story. 'What do you mean your grandma's not here any more?' he asked, not quite sure if he really wanted to know the answer.

'She died,' said the girl. 'A long time ago, on a big ship.'

Elliot swallowed. Was it really possible that this girl's grandma had died on the *Titanic*? On the ship he'd been on not a few hours ago? He struggled to do the maths in his head. He wasn't entirely sure when the *Titanic* had sunk but he knew from school that the Second World War had started in 1939. It didn't seem too wrong for the ship to have sunk some years before then.

Elliot felt sick and dizzy.

It was as though everything was fitting together but he couldn't work out quite why or how. He tried to go back over things in his head:

He'd found the ticket under his pillow.

His mum had played his grandma's tape.

And a dragon had come to fetch him.

The dragon that had come to fetch him was the toy that belonged to this girl.

But back in Bonn, when they'd met Beethoven, he'd been saved by another girl, who was also holding a green toy. The toy must have been Kimorin, so that girl must have been this girl's great-great-grandma.

And the woman who'd helped him on the *Titanic* had said she'd left behind a special guardian for her daughter. Could that have been Kimorin too?

The only thing that didn't quite fit was seeing his great-grandpa in Riga. What connection did he have to everything? He hadn't played Beethoven or been on the *Titanic*.

Elliot sighed.

What did it mean? Why did everything lead to this girl?

The girl watched Elliot curiously. He realised he'd been staring blankly into space, his eyes glazed over. There was something there, something just out of reach. What was it? What was he missing?

'Are you okay?' the girl asked.

'I think so,' said Elliot, bringing himself back to the dark room and the small girl. 'I lost my nan too. Or . . . I didn't lose her – she died. But everyone keeps saying that we lost her.'

'And everyone says they're sorry too,' said the girl. 'I hate that.'

'Yes!' said Elliot. 'I don't know why people keep saying sorry. It's not like they just knocked me over.'

'Or stole your sandwiches.'

'Or called me a dollop.'

The boy and the girl giggled.

When they were done, the girl's face turned serious.

'Could I play you a song I was writing?' she said. 'You can tell me what you think. It's not very good yet, because I've only just started. You can learn songs on a chalk piano, but you can't write anything on one because no sound comes out.'

Elliot nodded. He guessed this was where the envelope was going to appear. Who knew where it would lead next? Wherever it was, he wished it could wait a while so that he could spend a little longer with the girl. Something about her made sense to him. Like him, she seemed to get on better with music than she did with other kids.

The girl positioned her hands over the yellowing keys of the piano. Her fingernails had been bitten painfully short. Elliot had used to bite his too, before he'd started playing the violin. It was like there had been a buzzing energy that needed a way to get out.

She started to play.

A familiar team of four notes emerged from the piano.

She played the simple, rolling tune written by Grandma Ellen, the tune that had played on the tape what felt like years ago.

Elliot heard his own breathing falter and he stumbled backwards. The young girl glanced over her shoulder but didn't stop playing.

'Are you quite all right?' she asked.

Elliot wasn't sure how he had missed it this entire time.

'What did you say your name was?' he asked. His voice didn't sound like his at all.

'I don't believe I told you my name, which is rather rude of me, but you didn't tell me yours either.' The girl frowned. 'My name is Eleanor, but I don't really like it. So, everyone calls me Ellen.'

This little girl standing at the piano was his Grandma Ellen.

The thought hit him like an arrow.

His grandma had been a ten-year-old girl.

Now she was gone.

And Elliot was a ten-year-old boy.

And one day, he would be gone too.

He would be gone.

Not to sleep. Not to school. Not to anywhere.

Just gone.

No more hot chocolate.

And no more music.

And no more anything at all.

Just nothing, for ever, in all directions.

As the young Ellen continued to play, Elliot dashed madly for the door. He had no idea where he was going, but he knew he couldn't stay in that room. Not with the little girl who would become his favourite person in the whole word – his best friend – and then leave him for ever.

Not with the understanding that one day he would leave someone else all alone too. Who would it be? His friends? His children? He couldn't imagine being married, but most people got married and had children, didn't they?

Or maybe Elliot wouldn't leave anyone alone. Maybe Grandma Ellen was the one real friend he'd ever have. Maybe he'd grow up and be just as alone as he was now. No friends, no grandma, no music. The rest of his life would be exactly like school. People would either laugh at him or ignore him. No one would ever share a pair of earphones with him or go with him to concerts or ask him how a certain song made him feel as he was staring out of a train window.

Elliot ran as fast as his legs would carry him, along the narrow streets of the village. Baskets of bright flowers rocked as he passed them and lounging pigeons skittered out of his way, squawking.

He passed a butcher's and a cobbler's and a bakery.

They were the kind of shops his grandma had talked about, not the kind of shops that he'd ever actually seen. *None of these exist any more*, he thought. *These are all gone. Like I will be. Like everything will be.*

He ran until there was no feeling left in his feet and his lungs ached and his heart felt as though it was going to burst. At the side of the river, he slumped against one of the willows and sank to the ground. He wheezed.

Elliot felt tears begin to seep out of the corners of his eyes, blurring his vision. He dug his fingers into the grass and yanked up great big handfuls of turf. As though he was trying to dig to the other side of the world, Elliot scooped and tore chunks out of the ground, flinging them over his shoulder and into the river. He ripped and pulled until his hands turned brown and the seams of his fingernails filled with dirt. Lumps of rock buried themselves in his palms and the grass stained his skin green.

Eventually, exhausted, he stopped. He was surrounded by clods of dirt and shredded chunks of grass.

'Hey,' said a reedy, high-pitched voice.

Elliot jumped to his feet. There was no one here but him. He spun around but saw nothing except for the large willow tree. Could the tree be talking to him? he wondered. It seemed incredibly silly, but so did the idea of his ten-year-old grandma sitting at a piano nearby. Elliot felt his cheeks grow hot. He raised his hands to show that he was harmless and took a few steps away from the willow.

'Are you talking to me?' he asked the wizened old tree.

'Course I'm talkin' to you. Who else is there?'

'I didn't know trees could talk,' he said. 'I'm sorry I pulled up all that grass. I didn't mean to, I was just sad. Or not sad exactly, but afraid. I know that doesn't make much sense but—'

A bright, surprised laugh came from nowhere. 'You big mugglenut,' said the voice. 'Course it ain't the tree talkin' to you. Since when do trees talk, Olio? It's me. Your favourite dragon guardian, come to stop you doin' somethin' daft.'

Embarrassed, Elliot looked away from the tree. 'Kimorin?' he asked. The dragon wasn't anywhere around him, nor was he in the pink sky overhead. 'Where are you?'

'I'm down here.'

Elliot looked down at his feet to see the cuddly dragon that the girl had been holding back in the church hall. His dainty cloth feet were speckled with mud.

'It's actually you?' Elliot asked.

The tiny dragon nodded its head, the cloth tongue of flame flapping loosely out of its mouth. 'I know, I know,' he said. 'I ain't as handsome as normal. This is what you get when you disappear on me, Olio. I ain't got a choice but to follow you in the body of a Beanie Baby.'

Elliot grumbled. Now he was over the shock of seeing the dragon as a shrunken toy, he remembered how upset he was at his guardian. He frowned. 'What do you want, Kimorin?'

'To help you,' said the dragon softly. 'It's dangerous out there, Olio – you can't just go wanderin' off, specially not in your state. Remember what we talked about? If them Hushes steal your Spark, that's it. You'll never care about another song again.' The cloth flame in Kimorin's mouth flickered. 'So where to next, Olio?'

'I don't know,' said Elliot, scrunching his hands into fists. 'Away from here.'

Kimorin raised his stitched hands in frustration. 'But you ain't got an envelope!'

'Maybe I don't want an envelope.'

Kimorin tilted his tiny, hand-sewn face at Elliot. His mouth twitched and his eyes sparkled. For a second, Elliot had the distinct impression that the dragon was able to see inside his head, to somehow understand everything he was feeling. 'You can't be scared of death, Olio,' he said.

Elliot gulped. How had he known? Was it that obvious? 'Why not?' he asked.

The dragon flapped a wing, signalling for Elliot to come down to his level. Elliot crouched slightly.

'You can't be scared of death,' said Kimorin, ''cos you've already been there.'

The boy grunted impatiently. 'What does that even mean?'

'Stop askin' questions an' think about it,' Kimorin insisted. Elliot flared his nostrils defiantly. 'Listen, you weren't alive when the dinosaurs plonked about, were you?'

'No,' huffed Elliot.

'Or when Henry the Eighth chopped off his wives' heads or the Egyptians buried their pharaohs or Marco Polo ventured across the world in search of adventure?'

Elliot didn't see the point of this conversation. 'You already know I wasn't alive then!'

'And how did that feel?'

'I don't know, obviously,' Elliot said. 'I wasn't there.'

'Think, Olio.' Kimorin pointed to his head with an outstretched, plush claw. 'Did it hurt? Was it painful? Were you sad?'

'I wasn't anything.'

'Exactly!' exclaimed Kimorin. 'But you are somethin' right now, Olio. Matter of fact, you are much more than somethin'. You are a witness to the universe and everythin' in it! You can hear music and taste food and, most importantly of all, you can love someone so much that it feels like the end of the world when they go.' Elliot didn't say anything. That didn't sound like such an exciting position to be in. 'Imagine if you were a lamp or a pumpkin,' said Kimorin. 'You'd never have had the chance to listen to Beethoven or drink tea in the mornin' or ever meet your wonderful grandma!'

The mention of Grandma Ellen was too much. He thought of the little girl. His best friend. All the places in the world where his nan used to be.

'Maybe I want to be a pumpkin!' he shouted. 'Maybe I want to be a lamp! Specially if it means I never have to feel like this ever again!'

Elliot hated this painful feeling that had made itself at home in his chest. Every time he thought about Grandma Ellen, it hurt so much he couldn't bear it. He didn't want to hear about death any more. He wanted to be alone.

'Just . . . leave me alone.' He smudged the last of the tears into his cheeks, got to his feet and walked away.

*

Kimorin, who'd found himself with even shorter legs than usual, was in no position to give chase. Instead, he shimmied up the large willow tree so that he could get a better view of the boy he was supposed to be looking after.

He watched as Elliot's figure shrank before the young boy, hopped over a fence and disappeared into a wheat field. The ears of the crops quivered as the boy barrelled through them. He seemed to be moving in zigzags, totally unsure of where he was going.

The dragon sighed.

A wood encircled most of the field. Its trees were shaking, their leaves fluttering to the ground as though they were being torn off by a powerful wind.

Kimorin looked again.

There was no wind.

But something was stirring the leaves.

He blinked.

Large, familiar creatures swarmed out of the trees and into the field from every direction, trampling stalks beneath their heavy feet. A dank smell wafted through the air. Sinister roars echoed like crashing thunder between the hills.

The Hush-Hushes had come.

15

*E*lliot had broken into a sprint and was barrelling through tall stalks of wheat, when he collided with a wall of dirty hair. Falling on to his back, he let out a cry of terror at the sight of the Hush-Hush looming over him. He tried to scramble to his feet, only to bump into yet another heavy curtain of hair.

The Hush-Hushes stood in a circle around him, swaying gently like overgrown sea anemones. Elliot was completely surrounded. Before he could remember that they followed sounds so he should keep quiet, they'd closed in around him. Their lumpy ears twitched, out of place against their gargantuan bodies. They leaned over him, blocking out the sky entirely. There was no way for him to struggle, nowhere for him to go.

Clawed hands emerged from their filthy coats.

Elliot howled and shut his eyes, trying to block it all out. He wished he was back in his bed. He wished he was at home with Mum. He wished that Nan was still alive. He wished so hard it hurt.

The smell was more than just a smell this time. It became the entire world. Elliot could see nothing and hear nothing past that grisly, musty, ancient stink of earth and mud and meat and rot.

Scaly, flaky claws grasped at him from every angle. They pinched at his clothes and pulled at his hair. They scratched and scraped and poked and tore.

They took hold of his ears.

And then they moved past his ears.

Into his head.

It felt as though a large, heavy chest, holding every music note ever played, had been thrown open.

One by one, the Hush-Hushes were eating the notes.

They were stealing the music.

A blinding pain filled Elliot's head. When he tried calling out again, he made no sound at all. There was no song, no band, no Beethoven playing his sonata. There was no music there for him in his time of terror, not even the chirping tune of a robin.

Elliot was suddenly filled with regret. He should

never have left Kimorin behind.

Or run off without an envelope.

Or given up on music, so that the Hush-Hushes could come and take his Spark.

What would life really be like without music? Kimorin had said that a life without happiness and sadness would be boring, but a life without music would be even worse. Music had a way of helping everything make sense. Music had a way of turning feelings into things you could understand.

Elliot stopped being able to feel anything at all. He no longer had the vicious claws of the Hush-Hushes grabbing at him. There was nothing.

A deep, gritty voice spoke to Elliot from inside his own head.

'Do not struggle,' said the voice. 'We have you now.'

No, you don't, Elliot wanted to tell them.

'You have no use for this any more,' said the voice.

The voice was talking about his Spark, the way it felt when he listened to the songs he loved.

'You have no use for this any more,' said the voice again.

I do, Elliot tried to say. *I do.*

'You have no use for this any more,' said the voice a third time.

No! Elliot tried to shout. *Leave me alone!*
But there was only silence.

16

$\mathcal{E}$lliot Oppenheim woke in his own bed. He was neither warm nor cold. He was neither happy nor sad. He felt curiously empty, as though someone had scooped out all of his insides.

Everything was very quiet.

There were no birds singing in the trees outside.

All he could hear was the slow, tuneless ticking of a plastic clock on the wall.

What a strange dream, he thought.

Only then did he realise that something wasn't right. His room – and everything inside it – was grey. It was like being trapped in an old black-and-white film, the type that Grandma Ellen would watch on Sunday afternoons. Somehow, Elliot didn't feel particularly surprised. In fact, he didn't feel particularly . . . anything.

There were no posters on his walls, or pieces of sheet music, or ticket stubs from concerts he'd attended with Grandma Ellen. Elliot noticed all of this, but it didn't make him feel much at all. *Maybe this is just how things are*, he thought. *There's nothing that I can do about it now.*

He pressed his hands into the duvet lying over him. It felt incredibly heavy and took a great effort to push off his body. Once he'd managed to move it, he wondered why he'd bothered. What point was there in getting out of bed again? Well, he was up now and he had nothing else to do, he supposed.

He stood up.

The carpet under his feet felt like nothing.

Two steps forward, two steps back.

His footsteps echoed around the room, dull and hollow.

He turned slowly around a few times before coming to a stop.

For what could have been seconds, minutes or hours, Elliot stood in the middle of his grey room doing absolutely nothing. Thoughts passed through his head like tiny fish. They were simple thoughts. His memories had become hazy and difficult to catch hold of. All he could really do was look around him and take in what he saw.

The low bed.

The closed curtains.

The wardrobe that his mum had found on the street. (Hadn't they spent a day painting it lime green? Now it was as grey as everything else.)

On one wall hung a small, round mirror, surrounded by a brass rim that was supposed to make it look like the porthole in a ship. Elliot wandered over to it and observed his own image in the polished glass. The boy who looked back at him was as grey as a smear of ash.

Yes, he supposed that was how he looked.

Two eyes, two ears, a nose, a flat mouth.

He stood still for another ten thousand years.

Things were grey.

All things were grey.

Nothing happened.

Nothing at all.

Until he spotted something in the top right corner of the mirror. Where the back wall was being reflected, he could make out some marks, drawn on the plaster with green chalk. The marks looked like legless, armless stick-people, trapped behind bars. Getting closer to the mirror, he studied the marks.

What did the little sticks mean? They weren't words, he could tell that. And they didn't look like any of the other languages he'd heard of. Why had someone drawn them on his bedroom floor? He turned and walked towards them, intending to scrub them away.

He tripped.

Something was poking out from under his bed. A hard, black case, made of worn leather. It was almost familiar. Almost. The object was like a word stuck on the tip of Elliot's tongue.

He bent down, flipped the catches and lifted the lid.

Inside was a dusty violin, covered in fingerprints. Without thinking, Elliot slotted the instrument in under his chin and delicately lowered its bow on to the strings. He wasn't sure what he was doing, but some other part of his brain seemed to take control of his arms. He wasn't thinking, he was just doing. He shuffled closer to the chalk doodles on the wall and played:

No sound came out of the violin, but he felt something suddenly. Something sharp and warm in his chest. He played again and, like ripples in water, the notes fanned out in all directions, carrying on endlessly into the world. The tiny vibrations lent warmth to his hands.

He played the notes again. He could just about make out the sounds, but they sounded far away.

More warmth filled his hands, spreading up his arms to his elbows. It was a strange, almost painful feeling at first, like coming in from the freezing cold and plunging your hands into hot water. But the more he played, the more the feeling returned. He played the four notes, again and again, until his entire body had warmed up.

And he looked around the room.

This isn't right, he thought. *None of this is right.*

And he realised then that this wasn't his room, not really. It was just four walls and a bed. It didn't have any of the things that made him, well, him. If it was really his room, it would have his sheets of music and his ticket stubs and his posters. It would have his memories in it.

He gripped the violin tighter and carried on playing.

Memories came back to him. Real memories, bursting with life and colour.

Last Christmas, when Grandma Ellen had taken him to see the Recycled Orchestra: an entire band of young people from Paraguay who'd built instruments using rubbish from the garbage dump they lived beside.

That summer morning when Grandma Ellen had come to the house at six a.m., woken Elliot and taken him for breakfast ice cream at the trucker café on the dual carriageway.

The time the church asked if she'd play for their harvest festival and they'd done a duet, playing side by side under a striped gazebo.

And then he remembered the Hush-Hushes, descending on him as he ran from Kimorin into the field of wheat. He remembered their claws digging into his head.

The happy memories evaporated, leaving Elliot behind in his silent, grey bedroom.

They'd taken his Spark. They'd closed in on him and stolen the music from inside his head. After that, the colour had gone from the world. What did that mean? Would he really never truly hear music again?

Would the rest of his life be spent hearing only the tick of the clock and the echo of his footsteps?

Panicking, Elliot shouldered open his bedroom door. He expected to see the narrow upstairs corridor of his terraced house. He expected to see the bathroom door and the stair rail and the framed photograph of his mum as a teenager, holding a tennis racket like a guitar.

But he didn't see any of that.

What waited outside Elliot's bedroom door was a desolate wasteland, as grey as his bedroom.

17

Thick banks of snow stood like frozen waves on the rocky slopes. Dense, slow-moving clouds hovered low in a sky the colour of tarmac. There was no sun, no stars, no moon. In the distance, the peaks of sharp, black mountains shaped the horizon. A vicious wind spun across the freezing ground, gathering crystals of ice and dust, rattling like a broken motor.

Elliot clung on to his violin, trying not to panic.

Where could I possibly be now? he thought. *Why can't I just go home?*

He'd thought he had felt alone before but right then, as he stood in the frame of his bedroom door, Elliot Oppenheim felt as though he was standing at the very edge of the world. Everything good and warm and happy was long behind him. All that stood ahead was endless cold and snow.

He had given up and let the Hush-Hushes steal his Spark. He had let them win.

And now he was completely and utterly lost.

Gusts of icy air scraped against Elliot's face. His nose, ears and hands throbbed in the chill. He turned to go back into his bedroom, out of the wind, but the door was gone. Only the skeleton of a tree stood alone and trembling, its branches stripped of any leaves. There was no way back. There was no way home.

Not knowing what else to do, Elliot tucked the violin back under his chin and continued to play. He played the song that had been written on his bedroom wall, the song that had been written by his grandma as a child and recorded by her as an old woman. The song contained the notes he'd heard in Bonn and on the *Titanic* and in the wood deep in the forest. They were notes that had been plucked out of the air by so many of his ancestors before him to keep them company in times of trouble.

As he played, the warmth again flooded back to his fingers, then his arms, then his chest, then his head. He stamped his foot in time to the vibrations he could feel in his fingertips. He couldn't hear anything but the whistle of the wind, and it didn't matter.

He felt something.

He lost himself in the music entirely. Alone in a strange land, Elliot let the music take hold of him. He couldn't hear but he could remember; he could conjure the sound of the notes in his head as he bowed them. There was comfort in the melody. He knew where it went and it took him with it. He could hide there. Playing made his body hum and scared away the bitter cold of the snowy desert.

After playing until his hands ached, Elliot let the violin drop from under his chin.

He opened his eyes.

He screamed and stumbled, almost falling on to his back.

A Hush-Hush was standing in front him. It was tiny, around the size of a cello, and bobbing happily from side to side. Unlike the larger creatures of its kind, the little Hush-Hush wasn't yet filthy. Its silky hair hung from it like the coat of a carefully groomed sheepdog. A few wooden beads had been threaded on to its hair. Compared to the adults, the creature looked almost cute, like an overgrown guinea pig or some new kind of Pokémon.

He noticed that the Hush-Hush's ears were pinker, fresher-looking ears than the others of its kind. He guessed that it was only young. Still, he didn't want to find out what kind of damage it was capable of inflicting.

'Please,' said Elliot, raising the violin in front of him like a shield. 'Don't hurt me. They already stole my Spark. I don't have anything left.'

'Mmm,' purred the creature, its voice echoing inside Elliot's head like a thought. 'Don't . . . steal . . . music. . .'

'Then what do you want?' asked Elliot, lowering his instrument.

'Mmm . . . listen . . . music . . . mmm.'

Elliot let himself relax slightly. The creature didn't seem like it meant him any harm. It hadn't tried to get inside his head and, even if it did try, Elliot was sure he'd be able to outrun it.

'Where are we?' he asked, pointing to the barren landscape around them with his bow.

'Mmm . . . home . . .'

'This is where you live?' asked Elliot, his teeth chattering. 'It's so cold. Is this where all Hush-Hushes come from?'

'Mmm . . .' said the creature, which Elliot took to mean yes.

'Is it always like this?' Elliot knew that Kimorin would tell him off for asking so many questions if he were here. But the little Hush-Hush didn't seem to mind.

'Mmm . . . always . . . mmm . . . winter. Always . . . cold.'

'Do you know how I can get home?' said Elliot. 'I live at number four, Owlwood Drive. Usually I find a ticket to *The Night Train*, but this time I sort of ran away before it appeared.'

'Mmm . . . don't . . . know . . . home . . . mmm . . . train . . . night . . .'

'What about an envelope?' said Elliot. 'Have you seen an envelope anywhere?' He wondered if it knew what an envelope was. 'It's like a folded-up piece of paper with another piece of paper inside it.' The Hush-Hush stared at him blankly. 'Envelope?' he said again. 'Paper?' He mimed sliding a letter into an envelope, licking the seal and closing it. 'Have you seen one?'

'Mmm . . . food?' said the Hush-Hush.

Elliot sighed. 'No, not food.' He took a seat on a jagged hunk of rock and laid his violin across his lap.

The little thing moved closer. 'Nice . . . music . . .' it said, purring. 'Pretty . . .'

'Thanks,' said Elliot. 'You're really not going to try and steal my Spark?'

'Hush-Hush . . . don't . . . mmm . . . steal . . . Spark . . .'

'Are you sure?' said Elliot. 'Because I'm pretty sure they do. Ever since I walked through my wardrobe, that's literally all they've tried to do. Wherever I go, they start appearing and trying to get inside my head and steal my Spark, which is apparently what makes you care about music in the first place.'

'Don't . . . mmm . . . eat . . . Spark . . .' It sounded firm this time.

'All right,' said Elliot, holding his hands up in surrender. 'Agree to disagree, if you want. But I'm pretty sure a hundred of your relatives just climbed inside my head and stole all the music. Now I can't hear anything I play. All I can hear is your weird voice in my head. I can't even hear my own voice if I sing. Listen to this.' He stood up and cleared his throat. 'BAH FAR LOG LOO!' he sang. The little creature flinched. 'See?' said Elliot. 'I didn't hear a thing.'

The boy and the Hush-Hush sat in silence. The sky was growing dark, its heavy clouds sinking towards the ground. Elliot wondered whether it would get even colder as it grew darker.

'It's . . . mmm . . . so . . . cold . . . Hush . . . home . . .'

Despite himself, Elliot was starting to get frustrated by the slow, strange voice of the baby Hush-Hush. 'Yeah,' said Elliot. 'I know, I'm here. I can feel it.'

'If . . . people . . . mmm . . . don't . . . need . . . music . . . no more . . . mmm . . . we . . . take . . . Spark . . . so . . . mmm . . . we . . . can . . . listen . . . music too.'

Elliot couldn't believe what the Hush-Hush was trying to tell him. 'You want Sparks so you can listen to music?' he asked. The thought had never occurred to him. 'You steal other people's music so you can listen to it?'

'Mmm . . . music . . . makes . . . everything . . . mmm . . . warm . . .'

The boy wasn't particularly convinced. 'You're really trying to tell me that you're not baddies? That you only take Sparks to keep yourselves alive?'

'Mmm.'

'But they got inside my head!' shouted Elliot. 'They cornered me and pinned me down and made it so I can't hear any notes! It was horrible.'

The creature didn't look at all frightened by Elliot's

shouting. In fact, it moved closer to him, as though unsure that the boy had been able to hear what it had been saying.

'You . . . don't . . . want . . . Spark . . . no more . . . mmm . . .'

'People are allowed to change their minds!' objected Elliot, his teeth chattering. 'You can't just make it so they never *enjoy* music again. That's not fair.'

The Hush-Hush made a gurgling sound. 'So . . . you . . . want . . . music . . .?'

'Yes!' shouted Elliot. 'Yes, I want music! Okay? Obviously I do. Obviously I don't want to spend for ever without music.'

'You . . . want . . . music . . .' said the creature, tilting its head.

'I don't know if anyone's ever told you this,' said Elliot. 'But it's really annoying to just repeat what other people say, especially when you do it so slowly.'

The Hush-Hush's pink ears twitched. 'Go . . . to . . . music . . .'

'I don't know what you're talking about,' said Elliot. 'And I'm really starting to get cold. I don't know if I have the energy to play anything else, I'm sorry.'

'Music . . . mmm . . .'

The creature shuffled over to Elliot and nudged him with its head. He tried pushing it away, but even though it was a quarter of the size of its relatives, the little Hush-Hush had a surprising amount of strength.

'Hey,' said Elliot. 'Stop it.'

'Mmm . . . music . . .'

It headbutted Elliot in the knees, knocking him backwards into the snow. If Kimorin were here, he would have found it all hilarious. Elliot stood and brushed the snow off with his painfully frozen hands.

'Mmm . . . music . . .' it said again.

'Yes,' said Elliot. 'I get it. Mmm music. Now stop it. I'm not playing again.'

'Music . . . us . . . come . . .'

The creature had taken a few steps forward and then turned back to Elliot.

Elliot frowned. 'Wait,' he said. 'Do you want me to follow you?'

The hairy thing nodded eagerly. Elliot took a deep breath. Was it the worst idea in the world to follow a Hush-Hush into a snowy wilderness? Would it almost definitely lead him somewhere so that its parents could eat him whole? What if they liked the taste of his Spark so much that they'd sent it out to find more? It couldn't really be true that they took your Spark just to listen to music, could it?

You're asking too many questions again, Olio.

Elliot looked around him at the wasteland and shivered. The relentless wind chased ice crystals around his ankles. The dark clouds sank lower and lower. Somewhere in the distance, he heard the ticking of the plastic clock.

What other choice did he have? If he didn't go, he would freeze here anyway.

'Fine,' he said, getting to his feet. 'I'll come with you. But this had better not be a trap.'

'Mmm,' said the small creature, shuffling through the snow.

The boy followed the young Hush-Hush towards the distant black mountains.

18

It was difficult terrain for Elliot to move across, especially clutching a fragile old violin to his chest. The clothes and boots that the conductor had given him had been comfortable on the train, but in the land of the Hush-Hushes, they were virtually useless. The frosty breeze filled his trousers. The hairs in his nostrils grew stiff with ice. His breath rolled out of his mouth like smoke.

The Hush-Hush kept leaving Elliot behind. Every now and again, it would realise that it couldn't hear the boy's footsteps any more, and loop back to look for him. Elliot would generally be sitting on the ground, looking like someone who was more than ready to give up.

'Got . . . to . . . mmm . . . move . . .' the Hush-Hush would say.

And Elliot would carry on.

Elliot's eyelashes froze. His feet grew heavier and heavier in their flimsy shoes, until it felt like they had turned to lead. The clouds that had been in the sky a few hours earlier were now so low that the boy and the Hush-Hush were walking through them.

It soon became difficult to see anything at all.

If the Hush-Hush went more than a few steps ahead, Elliot became completely unable to make him out. He was guided by the trail of the creature's wide, star-shaped footprints in the mucky snow.

If Kimorin had been there, he was sure he wouldn't be slowly turning to a block of ice. Elliot realised that he missed the dragon and his endless chatter.

Why couldn't he have forgiven the dragon? It wasn't like he'd actually tried to do anything mean to Elliot. They'd got separated and then he'd come back to help. Elliot had been angry, and he'd let the anger decide what to do. Now the anger had gone, he was left in a frozen wasteland with no music, no plan and no feeling in his fingers.

'How much longer do we have to walk?' Elliot asked.

'Mmm . . . music . . .'

'Really helpful,' muttered Elliot. 'Thank you.'

'Mmm . . .'

'You can't breathe fire, can you?'

'Mmm . . .'

'Didn't think so.'

As they carried on, he realised something: the Hush-Hush didn't smell. If it had done, he'd have been able to sense it approaching him back when he was playing his violin. But it had virtually no smell at all. Perhaps, he thought, they didn't start smelling until they got older. Until they started eating Sparks.

'Can I ask you something?' said Elliot. 'It might sound rude.'

'Mmm . . .' said the Hush-Hush inside his head.

'How come you don't smell? Whenever I met other things like you, they always smelled . . . bad.' He didn't know how else to describe it to the little creature.

'Smell . . .?' said the Hush-Hush, as though it was an entirely new word.

'Yeah,' said Elliot. 'You know, like smell . . . bad. Smell like old fish and socks. Stinky smell.'

'No . . . music . . . no . . . bath . . .'

'I don't understand.'

'Mmm . . .'

Elliot decided to leave it at that, the cold making him tired.

They carried on up a steep sheet of crumbling rock that led to a narrow passage running between two of the black mountains. The passage was barely wide enough for Elliot to fit through with his belly sucked in. He wondered how any of the fully-grown Hush-Hushes ever managed to make their way along it.

At either side, cracked grey rock climbed for ever upward like the walls of a forgotten castle. Ahead, there was no end in sight, just an apparently never-ending stretch of rocky road. Elliot began to wonder whether they were actually going anywhere at all, or whether the Hush-Hush that was supposed to be leading him was as lost as he was.

'Kimorin!' he shouted, knowing that it would be absolutely no use. 'Are you out there?'

'Mmm . . . yes . . .' said the Hush-Hush.

'Not you,' Elliot said gently, not wanting to hurt the young creature's feelings.

'Mmm . . .'

The passage came to an abrupt halt. On each side, narrow steps had been cut into the rock. Elliot glanced nervously up but he couldn't see a place where the steps finished. They rose into the clouds and disappeared. It was a treacherous climb and Elliot spent most of it trying his best not to look down.

He had never liked climbing. When other kids talked about wanting to climb trees, he could never understand why they wouldn't rather sit in their shade with a pair of headphones on. What was the pointing in climbing up when you'd only have to climb back down again?

The steps eventually came to an end at a narrow platform, affording a wide view of the cloud-covered land and the grim sky watching over it. From there, a gap in the rock let them into a chamber in the side of the mountain. The ceiling was low. Stalactites and stalagmites pointed to each other like teeth in a giant's jaw.

The deeper they went, the less room they seemed to have, until Elliot was forced to crawl on his hands and knees. He remembered a word his grandma had used once: claustrophobic. They'd been in an elevator going to visit one of her friends when it had broken down.

I'm feeling claustrophobic, Nan had said. *Won't you sing to me and take my mind off it until someone gets us out?*

He hadn't really wanted to but he had noticed how

uncomfortable she looked about being stuck in that tiny space and so he'd stood with his hands behind his back and sung 'There Is a Light That Never Goes Out' as best as he could.

Elliot shivered. His knees bruised as they dragged along the rocky floor of the cave.

It became darker.

And colder.

And Elliot crawled on.

Until it became less dark.

And less cold.

And they emerged in a vast cavern with a ceiling so high Elliot couldn't be sure it wasn't just another sky.

At its centre, a huge, warm, grey fire was blazing. The flames cast dancing shadows on the walls. By the flickering light, Elliot could make out countless images, carved into the stone. Even in the cave, everything was colourless.

In a ring around the fire sat hundreds of Hush-Hushes. Some wide, some narrow, some tall, some short, all covered in stringy, matted fur. Now he'd been to their homeland, the fur made sense; the creatures were just trying to keep warm.

Thousands of ears turned to Elliot and the Hush-

Hush as they entered the packed cave. Elliot fought the urge to run. If the little one said they didn't actually eat Sparks, then maybe he could get his own back. Besides, he wasn't about to venture back out into the freezing cold and climb down a mountain when there was a roaring fire right in front of him.

The little Hush-Hush ambled forward.

The others rose up.

For a few minutes, they stood facing each other, swinging their arms and twitching their ears. Elliot couldn't hear any of what they said but he guessed by the way the creatures were jostling and jabbing at each other that a conversation was taking place. The Hush-Hushes seemed to be debating something. Elliot hoped the little Hush-Hush wasn't getting in any trouble for bringing him back to their home. As his fingers and toes thawed out in the warmth, he was realising that had the creature not found him, he might not have lasted too much longer in the cold.

'What are you telling them?' asked Elliot. 'You're not telling them to eat me, are you?'

'Tell . . . them . . . you . . . want . . . Spark . . . mmm . . . back . . .' came the Hush-Hush's voice inside his head.

'Do you really think they'll say yes? If not, I can just

go.' Maybe he could start his own fire somewhere, though he wasn't hopeful.

The Hush-Hush made a sound as if to shush Elliot and the boy complied, deciding to bask in the warmth of the fire in case he was sent back out into the cold.

A decision appeared to have been reached. The Hush-Hushes went still. Elliot held his breath. For a second, the only thing to move in the cavern was the fire.

One of the tallest Hush-Hushes stood up. Its head touched the ceiling of the cave. A pair of spiny hands emerged from its coat, reached down and parted the shaggy hair that fell from the tip of its body to the ground.

A miniature Hush-Hush tumbled out. This Hush-Hush was even smaller than the one that Elliot had met out in the snow. It was the size of a cat and covered in fine, spiky fur, so short that you could still see its luminescent pink skin beneath. The little thing's tongue shot out of its mouth and ran up and down its hair. Elliot wasn't sure whether he found it cute or slightly gross.

The creature tottered towards him. It moved uncertainly, like a baby that had just learned how to walk.

It stopped a few feet from Elliot.

'Mmm . . .' said the baby Hush-Hush, jiggling like a jester at Elliot's feet.

Elliot stared at it, unsure of what to do.

'Go . . . closer . . .' said the Hush-Hush that had found him.

Elliot hesitantly dropped to his knees so that he was level with the small creature. The Hush-Hush scurried over to him, leaped into his hands, and opened its mouth.

At first Elliot couldn't hear anything but a bright light rushed at his face, and he squeezed his eyes shut. Gradually, he began to make out notes leaving the Hush-Hush's mouth and the music wrapped itself around him like a warm blanket. He could feel the songs he loved washing over him. They carried all kinds of feelings with them, some strange and some sad, some happy and some thoughtful, some simple and some complicated.

He opened his eyes.

Suddenly, colour swept back into the world.

The fire became a shimmering, orange tangle of flame.

The Hush-Hushes became a mucky patchwork of browns, greens, greys and yellows.

Even Elliot's own hands regained their colour, and he could see how painfully red and tender they had become in the bitter cold.

Now that colour had returned to everything, his attention was caught by the pictures on the walls. The drawings all seemed to show human beings. The majority of them looked unhappy. Some sat with their heads in their hands; some lay with duvets pulled up to their chins. Some were destroying instruments. In one, an old man with a flowing beard took a hammer to a grand piano. In another, a young girl beat her flute against a brick wall. Were these other people that had given up on music? People who had decided they didn't care any more, so the Hush-Hushes had been able to take their Sparks?

Elliot realised, then, that the Hush-Hushes didn't steal anything. They didn't need to. When people lost their love for music, the creatures simply took the Sparks that they were no longer using.

Elliot tilted his head back and took a deep breath.

Directly overhead was a crude sketch of Beethoven. Elliot would have recognised that face anywhere. It was on the cover of all the recordings and sheet music Grandma Ellen had of his. It was also the face of the crying boy he'd seen, pushed up to the piano by his father all those years ago.

Remembering what had just happened, Elliot smiled at the little Hush-Hush that had given him back his Spark. It scurried away, back to its parent.

'Thank you,' Elliot said, turning to the Hush-Hush who had led him to their cave. 'Please tell them all thank you.'

They all murmured in response.

'Mmm...' said the Hush-Hush. 'It...is...okay...'

'And I'm sorry for thinking that you all steal Sparks,' he added with slight embarrassment. 'I can see that you only take them when people stop using them. And I understand why you need music now.'

'Don't...mmm...eat...Sparks...'

'Yes,' said Elliot. 'That's what I said.'

Elliot grinned gratefully at the creatures. But his joy at finding colour and sound back in the world quickly fizzled out.

Even if he could hear again, it didn't mean *he* was any closer to getting back home. What was he supposed to do – live with the Hush-Hushes for the rest of his life? His mum was still at home and she would be worried sick about him by now. It didn't matter what

Kimorin had said about being outside of time. Surely it was at least morning by now?

And, he realised with a start, it would be Grandma's funeral soon.

If he wasn't there, Mum would have to face it alone.

'You . . . mmm . . . sad . . .?' asked the little Hush-Hush, noticing the look of distress on Elliot's face.

'I still don't know how to get home,' explained Elliot. 'I don't have a ticket. I don't know what to do.'

'Mmm. We . . . know . . .' said the creature cheerfully.

'You do?' Elliot asked uncertainly. Did the Hush-Hush really understand that Elliot meant his *own* home?

'We . . . mmm . . . sing . . .'

19

The Hush-Hushes joined hands around the fire. Elliot stood between the little creature that had led him in from the cold and the even smaller one that had given him back his Spark. Their clawed hands were surprisingly soft and strangely warm. It was like holding on to two hot water bottles.

All at once, the Hush-Hushes burst into song.

It wasn't a song in the same sense as the pieces written by Beethoven or Grandma Ellen or anything else Elliot had ever heard.

This was more like a deep, endless hum. It was like the sound of the earth itself waking up. Like the sound of time being put into reverse and stars forming and galaxies spinning in space.

The voices of the Hush-Hushes harmonised with

each other perfectly. They took it in turns to sing high and low and to wander off on beautiful solos that meandered unpredictably like mountain paths. Somehow, the creatures managed to create the full, rich, sweeping sound of an orchestra with only their voices.

Elliot felt the soles of his feet vibrate with the sound. The hairs on the back of his neck stood on end.

It was like being bathed in sound.

Wait, he thought, *it really does feel like being bathed in sound.*

Elliot looked from Hush-Hush to Hush-Hush. He couldn't help but laugh. This was what the little one had meant, earlier, when he'd asked about the smell. Somehow, they were actually being washed by the song. As they took it in turns to fly off on solos, the coats of the Hush-Hushes transformed from their murky, muddy colours to a white as bright as fresh milk. Singing together cleared away the dirt. A song had the same effect on Hush-Hushes as a warm bath did on a child who'd spent the whole day playing football in the mud.

Elliot glanced at his own hands and was amazed to see his fingernails clear of dirt.

'Mmm . . .' said the little Hush-Hush. 'Clean . . .'

Elliot could hardly believe it.

The freshly washed Hush-Hushes around him sparkled like snowmen.

'Sing . . .' said the Hush-Hushes. 'Sing . . .'

Though his voice was nowhere near as low as even the smallest Hush-Hush, Elliot tried his best to join in. He opened his mouth and released a high, warbling E, which mingled with the pulsing notes of the hairy creatures surrounding him. Singing with them felt like being accepted into something larger than himself. It was difficult to believe he'd been so terrified by the Hush-Hushes.

Or that a few hours before, he'd felt more alone than he'd ever thought possible.

He sang and he sang.

And, for a moment at least, he forgot a few sad things.

And remembered a few happier things.

And finally, he spotted it.

Peeking out from beneath the coat of the smallest Hush-Hush was the corner of an envelope. He tapped the creature and pointed to it. It looked down. It seemed surprised to see the paper and gladly passed it to Elliot, who turned it over in his hands. There was no doubt about it: this was a ticket to *The Night Train*. Maybe even a ticket home.

Clutching the envelope to his chest, Elliot took one last look at the band of singing Hush-Hushes, crammed together in the cave. Though they were miles from anyone else, stuck in the middle of an utterly desolate wilderness, the music tied them together. It gave them a moment outside of time. It washed them and it warmed them and it lit them up.

He could see that; he could feel it.

Music wasn't the thing you ran away from; it was the thing you ran away to. It was the place where things weren't broken, the place where things stayed the same. It was your ticket to the heart of the universe.

He felt a smile pushing up at his cheeks. The first real smile he'd felt in a while.

'Thank you,' he told the little Hush-Hush that had found him.

'Mmm . . . thank . . . you . . . mmm . . . too . . . for . . . violin . . . music . . .' The little creature said, and Elliot knew that under all of that fur, the creature must be smiling.

Elliot squeezed the Hush-Hush's soft hand.

Taking a breath, he ripped open the envelope.

And he disappeared.

20

'What's happening?' screamed Elliot.

The envelope hadn't whisked him into his cabin on *The Night Train*. Instead, he was hanging off the back of the end carriage by his fingertips. The speed of the train meant that the night was rushing at him with full force. His clothes fluttered like flags in a storm.

'Help!'

A familiar face appeared over the edge of the train. It was Kimorin, trying his best to look as though he had everything completely under control. The plumes of smoke curling out of his ears told Elliot he wasn't feeling quite as relaxed as his smile claimed.

'Stay calm, Olio,' said the dragon. 'You picked up your ticket a little later than you were meant to, so you didn't quite catch the train.'

'I can't hold on much longer!' Elliot shouted. 'Help me!'

The dragon tutted as though Elliot was asking for another biscuit after having just eaten six. 'Olio, you can hold on for much longer than you think you can. Trust me, I've held on to lots of things for way too long. Just wait there a sec while I find somethin' to pull you up with.'

The dragon scuttled backwards, out of sight.

'Don't go!' Elliot pleaded.

The feeling hadn't yet come back to his fingers and holding on felt impossible. His little finger slipped from the painted metal of the speeding carriage and Elliot could do nothing but watch in horror as his fingers continued, one by one, to slide off the back of the train.

'Kimorin!' he shouted, panic turning his voice into a high-pitched squeak.

'All right, all right,' muttered the dragon, his face reappearing overhead. 'You didn't think I was goin' to up and leave, did you?' He was carrying a lasso of black wire around one of his wings. 'Had to rip this off some kinda motory-lookin'-thing; hopefully it weren't too important. Get ready now.'

Kimorin took a couple of steps back, whipped the cable into orbit over his head, then slung it towards Elliot. 'Catch!' he bellowed.

Elliot let go of the train with one hand and thrust it as high as he could into the air. With a reassuring thwack, the cable landed in his palm and he gripped it.

'Both hands!' shouted Kimorin. 'I'll pull you up.'

Biting down to keep from screaming in terror, Elliot let go of the train completely and gripped on to the cable with both hands.

As Kimorin began to pull him up, the train hit a bump in the track and rocked, sending the cable – and Elliot with it – swinging wildly from the back of the carriage to its side.

Elliot tried to scream, but the terror had blocked his throat. He glanced up and saw a cabin window above him. On the other side of the glass, several passengers were playing a lilting folk song together, totally oblivious to the boy flailing desperately outside their window. Elliot tried to pull himself up so that they would see him but he was almost out of strength. He reached out to knock on the glass and his fingers barely grazed the bottom of the window.

'Don't let go!' shouted Kimorin.

'Why would I let go?' screamed Elliot, finding his voice.

The boy felt the cable sliding through his hands like wet soap. Elliot started to swing on the cord, trying to gain enough momentum to haul himself up on to the roof. The last of his energy was quickly ebbing away.

As he swung, the bottom of his foot grazed the rail. Sparks flew into his eyes. 'Oh no,' Kimorin groaned. 'Hurry! You have to hurry, Olio!'

Elliot looked ahead, in the direction the train was travelling. He felt his heart stop. They were approaching a tunnel.

His sweaty hands were wrapped around the very end of the cable. There was no way he would be able to climb up. Even if he could, there was no time.

The tunnel loomed, its ring of darkness advancing on the train like the mouth of a hungry beast.

'What do I do?' he screamed.

He could make out the cracks in the bricks of the tunnel. There was nothing else he could do.

Elliot let go of the cable.

He fell.

And then he rose again.

He rose until he was high above the train and the

tunnel, face to face with a shining, yellow moon.

Elliot was on the back of the dragon.

Relief washed over him like warm water.

'I thought you didn't give rides,' he told Kimorin.

'Just don't tell no one,' said the dragon. 'Else everyone will be wantin' one.'

*

They flew in a lazy circle through the night sky, taking in the peaceful patch of countryside that spread out below them. A river wound across ridged fields and lonely farms. Large ponds showed the moon its own face.

Below them, *The Night Train* emerged from the other side of the tunnel. It whistled, sending plumes of smoke towards the stars.

Kimorin tilted his wings. The boy and the dragon shot downwards, landing with a gentle thump on the roof of *The Night Train*. Kimorin unfolded one wing, which Elliot slid down like a slide.

'Thanks,' said Elliot.

'No sweat,' said the dragon. 'But we ain't safe yet, Olio. Let's get ourselves back in the warm, shall we?'

Keeping low, the boy and the dragon climbed along the roof of the train until they came to the gap between

two carriages. There, they took it in turns to drop down and throw themselves through the door.

Elliot breathed a sigh of relief.

It was warm and cosy in the carriage. Everything was how he remembered it. The plush carpet. The warm lanterns. The photographs of musicians, lost in their songs. Even the giant conductor was waiting for them, standing with his cap in his hand and a patient smile hovering between his ears.

'Cutting it fine this evening, aren't we, chaps? I did warn you about being late.'

'Sorry,' said Elliot. 'I couldn't find an envelope.'

'Quite all right – you're here now, are you not?'

'We are indeed,' said Kimorin. 'But you might wanna work on your safety features, big man.' He tossed the loop of cable into the conductor's hands. The giant looked down at it with amused surprise.

'We shall look into it immediately,' he replied.

'Ta very much,' said Kimorin, turning to Elliot. 'Now shall we get our backsides back to 444F and take a look at our next ticket?'

Back in the cabin, they took their usual seats. The train passed the ruins of a castle, lit up in silver by the full moon. Somewhere in the distance, a dog howled.

The blinking lights of a plane stuttered through the night sky.

Elliot took a moment to appreciate the warmth and the light and the soft, comfy seat under his tired legs. He reached up into the luggage rack and pulled down two freshly washed blankets. One he tossed to the dragon. The other he wrapped around himself. He kicked off his shoes and drew his feet in underneath him.

'Sorry for shouting at you,' he said to the dragon. 'I didn't mean any of it. I'm lucky to have you as my guardian, Kimorin.'

Kimorin grinned, showing off his huge teeth. He shook the blanket open across his lap. 'That's all right, Olio. But somethin' you gotta learn is that nobody is gonna be able to make your life perfect.' Elliot bit his lip. 'Would I have liked to keep you snug as a bug in a rug? Sure. Was it ever gonna be possible? No. You gotta give people some slack, Olio. Things don't go perfect. Great-grandads walk into forests, people drive into icebergs, little girls with pianos spook you. No dragon, no grandma and no friend is ever gonna be able to change that. All we can do is all we can do, Olio.'

'I know that now,' sighed Elliot, fidgeting with his blanket.

Kimorin smiled. 'You see, your grandma prolly did everythin' she ever could to keep you safe and happy, Olio. Most other people ain't gonna be like that. Even your bestest friends have their own lives to think about. They're as important to themselves as you are to you. Which ain't good and it ain't bad, it just is.'

'But that doesn't really matter,' said Elliot. 'Because I don't have any friends.'

Kimorin snorted, tiny jets of blue flame shooting from his nostrils. 'Olio, do you honestly believe that absolutely nothin' in your life is gonna change? You think that how things are when you're ten is gonna be how things are for ever?'

'Maybe they will,' said Elliot. 'Some things stay the same.'

'Think, Olio, when your grandma was your age, the world was at war, and nobody even had a TV at home. Now look. Everyone's electric scooterin' around with magic phones in their jeans and invisible headphones in their ears. Things change. That's the only thing that stays the same.'

'That sounded really smart,' said Elliot.

'I know,' said Kimorin. 'I heard a Roman emperor say it once and I stole it.'

They both fell into fits of giggles.

When they'd caught their breath, Elliot remembered something he'd wanted to ask his guardian about: that face he'd seen, back in the cave on the mountain.

'There was a picture of Beethoven on their wall,' said Elliot. 'The Hush-Hushes, I mean. I think they took his Spark.'

'They didn't take his Spark,' said Kimorin, swiping the air with his claw. 'He may have gone deaf and got sick and tired, but he never lost his Spark. You can tell that from his music. Music ain't about what you hear – it's about what you feel.'

'But why did they draw him?'

He shrugged. 'Could be that they're just fans, same as you, Olio.' The dragon leaned in to Elliot. 'Anyhow, what else did you see while you was visitin' with the Spark-stealers?'

'I saw babies,' said Elliot. 'And middle-sized ones. And lots of big ones.'

'The full band,' said the dragon.

'There was a fire too,' said Elliot. 'And lots of drawings of people being sad. And they sang together so that it sounded like . . . like a whole orchestra playing whatever they wanted but it all came together into one sound. I don't know how to explain it. It sort of sounded like everything.'

'Like everythin'?'

'Like a lot of things, at least.'

The dragon looked thoughtful. 'How did you manage to get yourself out in the end?'

Elliot felt something digging into his side. Lifting up the blanket, he realised that it was the corner of the envelope that he'd hurriedly stashed in his trousers. He drew it out and held it up for Kimorin to see. 'A Hush-Hush helped me and I found this.'

The boy and the dragon stared at it hopefully.

Elliot swallowed.

'What do you think it says?' he asked.

Kimorin let out an involuntary laugh.

'What's so funny?' asked Elliot.

'You coulda opened the envelope and found out what it was in half a second; instead, you wanted to ask me first. I know as much as you know, which is zero, unless you know more than I know, in which case there weren't much point in askin'. Remember what I said earlier?'

'"Questions ain't always the route to answers, Olio",' Elliot mimicked, rolling his eyes fondly. They both laughed and Elliot tore open the envelope.

The card inside was the same size and shape as the other tickets Elliot had received but that was where the resemblance stopped. Elliot squinted at it, trying to work out what it meant. He turned it over but the reverse side was blank. He turned it over again and frowned, not sure what he was supposed to do next.

'Well?' said Kimorin. 'Is it somewhere warm this time? Jamaica? Malawi? Australia? Don't leave me hangin', Olio. I'm gearin' up for a summer holiday over here.'

'It's not a ticket,' said Elliot, lowering the paper.

The dragon's face fell. 'Course it's a ticket. It ain't a watermelon. What else is it gonna be?'

Elliot turned the card around so that the dragon could read it. In the same curling, slanted writing as the tickets had been written in, the piece of card read:

Follow him.

'What does it mean?' asked Elliot.

'I suppose, Olio, that it means we follow him.'

Kimorin raised a claw as if to say: *Do not even think about asking another question.*

Elliot closed his mouth.

At that very moment, a shadow passed by the cabin window. It was a tall shadow, shaped like an adult man in a raincoat. The shadow of a man was clutching the shadow of a large case. Both shadows disappeared further down the carriage.

'I'm guessin' tha's our man,' said the dragon.

The Night Train juddered to a halt.

21

From behind, the man reminded Elliot of his great-grandad. He had the same broad shoulders, the same tufty hair, the same bold way of walking with his feet turned out.

Could it be his grandad, this time as an older man? Were they in the recent past now? Maybe even a time when Elliot was alive?

Whoever it was, the boy and the dragon followed him off the train and into the biggest train station Elliot had ever seen. Giant metal ribs held the glass ceiling up over more platforms than Elliot could count. Sleek, silver trains sat parked at the ends of their tracks. When Elliot looked closely, it seemed as though the trains were hovering a few centimetres off the rails. He shook his head, thinking he must just be tired.

Every free inch of the station was taken up by giant video adverts, playing on screens as thin as paper. They advertised things Elliot had never seen before: chewing gum that turned your hair blue, games with graphics you couldn't tell from reality, cruises around the dark side of the moon.

'Come on, Olio,' muttered Kimorin. 'We ain't got time to stand around gawkin' at nonsense.'

Each step they took echoed loudly through the empty station. Elliot felt sure that the man would hear them, but apparently he wasn't like his great-grandpa or the young Grandma Ellen. Or at least that's what Elliot thought until the man started bobbing his head up and down and it became clear that he had tiny earphones pressed into his ears.

The man didn't once look back.

As they left the station, Elliot caught sight of a row of bubbles, the size of small cars and as reflective as mirrors. They had no visible openings or joins. Like the trains, they seemed to be floating a few centimetres from the ground.

'Kimorin,' said Elliot, tapping his guardian's wing. 'What are those?'

'How do I know? Cars, probably. We're in the

future, Olio. About time too. You spend too long in the past, you start forgettin' there's anythin' else out there.'

They followed the man along a wide, slow-flowing river. Tiny, reflective pods bobbed on the water, similar to the ones they'd seen parked on the road. Elliot wondered whether in the future, cars could go on the land and on the water. Maybe they could even go into the sky too.

'It looks amazin',' said Kimorin, as though he could read Elliot's mind. 'But remember: you're livin' in someone's future too, and even these floatin' cars are someone's past.'

The man paused for a moment under the glow of a lamp post. He swiped his hand through the air and a rectangle of light appeared from nowhere. There were words written in the light and the man poked and flicked at them, shifting them around as though they were icons on a screen.

'Woah,' said Elliot.

'Woah?' said the dragon. 'I've flown around breathin' fire to rescue you, and never once did I get a "woah".'

Elliot blushed. 'I would have given you a "woah" if I

hadn't been so scared. I didn't know you wanted me to say "woah".'

The dragon burst into a laugh. 'I'm only pullin' your tiny leg, Olio. That thing's a million miles more interestin' than anythin' I can do. A phone that appears out of the air – imagine that.' The man swiped his hand and the screen disappeared. 'See?' said Kimorin. 'I told you everythin' changes. Phones, friends, cars. Ain't nothin' that stays the same.'

They carried on trailing the man as he wandered through the empty city. He seemed to be lost in thought and was humming under his breath to whatever music he was listening to. It wasn't familiar to Elliot. He guessed the music was from the future too. An urge came over him to rush over to the man, pull one of the earphones out of his ear, and listen in. He wanted to know what kind of songs people were writing in the years to come. Were there new kinds of music? New instruments? New ways of singing?

The tall man passed under a railway bridge. As the boy and the dragon followed him, a train rattled past overhead. Elliot wondered whether it was *The Night Train*. He remembered the face of the woman, Amina, who'd told him that she'd learned to cherish the things that reminded her of her husband, not to be afraid of them. Was she still sitting in one of the carriages? Had what she said been true? Could it be possible that every piece Elliot had ever played with his nan was just floating on endlessly through the universe? Perhaps in the future they had spaceships that travelled so far out you could hear all the sounds from the past. Not just his playing, but his nan's and his great-grandpa's and Beethoven's and even the dinosaurs, roaring and squawking as they stamped around the earth.

The man finally stopped walking outside a shabby-looking pub with its curtains drawn. A flaking sign identified it as The Merman. Below the pub's name was an incredibly detailed painting of a man reclining on a rock while waves broke around him. The man was long-haired and holding a flute to his lips. A gentle gust of wind sent the sign swinging.

The man plucked the earphones out of his ears and entered the run-down pub.

'Should we go in?' Elliot asked Kimorin.

'Well, we ain't gonna find anythin' out standin' here like a pair of dollops,' said the dragon.

Inside, they found themselves standing directly behind the tall man. He'd paused and was looking around himself in confusion. The pub appeared to be completely empty. Though a few lights were on and the slot machines were flashing, no one was behind the bar or sitting at any of the tables. It smelled of greasy food and sugary drinks. Faded illustrations of fish and dogs and Victorian cartoons hung from the walls.

Elliot wondered whether the man was, like them, outside of time. Maybe he just hadn't realised it yet.

The man put down the case he was holding and loosened his tie. He scratched the back of his neck.

'Hello?' he called out.

No one answered him. The place was spookily quiet.

'Is anyone there?'

All of a sudden, the room was completely filled with people as they leaped out from behind doors, below tables and under the bar, with paper hats on their heads and party horns in their mouths.

Handfuls of confetti were hurled into the air.

Party poppers burst like tiny fireworks.

The man threw his hands up in surprise and let out a scream that was somewhere between joy and terror.

People in party hats rushed towards him, singing.

'Happy birthday to you! Happy birthday to you!

Happy birthday, dear Elliot . . .'

Elliot felt his jaw drop.

He turned to the dragon, the realisation dawning on him.

'Kimorin?' he asked.

'Yes, Olio?'

'Is that . . .'

The dragon nodded. 'Correct, I think the man we've been followin', that tall, confused one blowin' out candles, might well be you.' He coughed. 'Happy birthday, Olio. Sorry I didn't get you anythin'.'

'But that's impossible!' said Elliot. He took a few steps forward, trying to get a better look at the man in the dim light. It was true that they looked slightly similar. They had the same colour eyes at least and the same dimples and the same kind of shaggy, auburn hair.

Elliot moved closer again.

He had Elliot's scar on his earlobe! The man was Elliot. The tall man with the hat and the invisible phone and the pub full of friends throwing him a surprise party was Elliot. It was too much to take in. The man looked so relaxed, so happy, and so . . . liked. People *liked* him. He had so many friends they barely fit into one pub. 'Impossible,' Elliot whispered again.

'Are we still callin' things impossible?' asked the dragon. 'I thought we stopped usin' that word around the time we met Ludwig van Beethoven and got chased by a yeti that wanted to make off with your Spark.'

'They don't steal Sparks!' said Elliot, tearing his attention away from the older version of himself. 'I mean, they do take them, but only if they think someone doesn't want music any more. Sorry, I meant to tell you earlier. When I met them, they explained everything. They just use our Sparks to listen to songs. They live in this cold, horrible, place, and they sing together to make themselves clean and warm.'

'Is that right?' asked the dragon, looking impressed that the boy had managed to discover so much.

'Yeah,' said Elliot. 'The little ones don't have their own way of listening to music, so their parents go and find Sparks for them. They only took mine because they thought I didn't want it any more. I thought I didn't want it any more either, but I was wrong.'

'So what made you change your mind, Olio?'

Elliot took a second to think. 'Even in the worst places, music was the thing that people had. Maybe it didn't make everything okay but at least it made them feel less alone or afraid or cold. And then it made me feel like that too.'

'You're right, Olio,' said Kimorin. 'It helps.'

'And I saw what it was like without music. Nothing felt like anything. It was all just grey. There was no story to any of it.'

Kimorin smiled. 'Music has a way of colourin' things in, whether they're happy or sad. It's the difference between a sketch and a painting.'

'Did a Roman emperor say that too?' asked Elliot.

'No,' said Kimorin proudly. 'A pukey dragon did.'

In the middle of the pub, the older Elliot had finished blowing out his candles. The friends huddled around him cheered and laughed and patted him on the back. He was beaming. Someone fixed a badge to his shirt that read 'Birthday Boy'. Someone else placed a paper hat on his head and pulled the elastic down under his chin.

Elliot realised he recognised some of the faces: there was his old music teacher, Mrs Lancet, still wearing a jumper covered in crisp crumbs. And there was Lewis, who now had his nose pierced and wore bright orange boots. And there was even a woman who, Elliot realised with a sharp jolt of shock, was his mum. Her hair was threaded with a little more silver and she seemed smaller somehow, but her eyes still sparkled and she applauded happily as she watched the older version of himself blushing.

A young woman with red hair pulled herself up on to the bar and shouted for some quiet. She held a glass of wine to her chest and looked down fondly at Elliot.

'I'd just like to say, as I'm sure you'll all agree, that we're thrilled to be celebrating the birthday of the only violinist ever to eat four cheeseburgers in one sitting.' The gathering cheered. The girl continued her speech. 'I remember when I first met Elliot. It was the first day of music college and he came in with headphones on, carrying the biggest hot chocolate I'd ever seen, which he proceeded to spill directly on to my white trainers.' Everyone laughed. The older Elliot blushed. 'And we've been best friends ever since. Elliot's not only one of the most talented people I know, he's also one of the kindest, one of the funniest, and one of the weirdest.' She raised her glass high. 'To Elliot Oppenheim, and his first thirty years on planet earth!'

'To Elliot Oppenheim!' echoed the other guests, raising their glasses too.

A song started to play from a speaker that had been

put up in one corner. Elliot recognised it straight away. It was a song he must have listened to more than a thousand times. It was a song he'd shared with Grandma Ellen, a song that both of them had loved so much they could sing it backwards.

'That's my favourite song!' shouted Elliot.

'Course it is,' said Kimorin. 'What else would they play at your surprise party?'

'They're my friends,' whispered Elliot to himself. 'I have friends.'

'Course you do,' said the dragon. 'So you got a little unlucky and didn't manage to find your tribe in school – just means you'll find 'em a bit later on. We all got people out there waitin' for us; it's just about trackin' 'em down.'

The two of them watched as the party guests proceeded to wander towards the area where the tables and chairs had been cleared away and start dancing.

The older Elliot, noticed the younger Elliot, didn't dance much different to how he danced now. He put his hands in the air and wiggled them from side to side as though he was trying to get the attention of a lifeguard.

Kimorin curtseyed in front of Elliot and held out his claw.

'Should we?' the dragon asked.

And they did dance, for a moment at least. But a boy and a dragon don't make the best of dancing partners and it wasn't long before Elliot was lying face down on the sticky floor and Kimorin was lifting him to his feet.

'We tried,' said Kimorin. 'Ain't nobody can say we're party poopers.'

'I don't think I like dancing,' said Elliot.

'And I don't think dancin' likes you.'

The boy giggled until his giggle became a yawn. He stretched his arms wide and stuck out his chest. His eyelids felt incredibly heavy. Oily dots and dashes swum past his eyes.

'Not borin' you, am I?' asked the dragon.

'No,' said Elliot. 'I've just been awake for so long. What time is it?'

'You ain't been up hardly a second, trust me. Time is but a distant memory to me an' you at this point.'

The woman with the red hair twirled past the two of them, icing from the cake smeared around her mouth. Clearly visible in the pocket of her threadbare jacket was a gleaming white envelope. Elliot waited until she passed back their way and he swiped the ticket. She

didn't notice a thing. Her eyes were closed, her arms were in the air and she was singing along with the other party guests.

Holding the envelope, Elliot shrugged at Kimorin. Neither of them said anything for a moment. The party picked up speed around them and the boy and the dragon fidgeted as though they weren't quite sure what to say. They both knew that their adventure was almost at an end. Elliot understood that the envelope in his hands would be the envelope that took him home.

'I think it's the one,' said Elliot.

'I think so too,' said the dragon.

'Goodbye, then, Kimorin,' said the boy.

'It's only goodbye if I disappear from inside your head,' said the dragon.

Elliot thought about that for a moment. 'I'm not going to forget you, if that's what you mean.'

'Well, then,' said Kimorin gently. 'I ain't hardly gonna be gone, am I?'

Still, the boy didn't open the envelope.

'Are we friends?' he asked.

'Course we're friends,' said the dragon. 'Me and you and this entire pub of truly awful singers. In the future and in the past, we're friends.'

'Thanks,' said Elliot.

'Thanks to you too. But not for that. Bein' friends ain't a favour – it's an honour.' The dragon winked. 'Now, go have a noisy life. Make music, make friends, make cake. I'll see you when I see you, Olio.'

And, for the last time that night, Elliot Oppenheim tore open a bright white envelope and disappeared.

22

*E*lliot Oppenheim awoke in his own bed. He lay still for a few minutes, taking in the sounds that were playing out around him.

Across the hallway, his mum was singing in the shower.

Outside the window, birds were performing solos on the stage of the old oak tree.

And in the corner of Elliot's room, the old tape machine was crackling, having run out of cassette to play.

Elliot opened his eyes.

He could hear music! More than that, he could *feel* it.

It was a bright, blue morning, the kind that promised a long, warm day. Even in his room, the air smelled of cut grass and flowers. Their neighbour was standing over her lawn, spraying it with water from a hose that split the morning sun into miniature rainbows.

Elliot kicked off the duvet and hurried over to the stereo. He pressed eject. Carefully, he lifted out the old, dusty tape that his mum had put in. A label had been stuck to one side. In spidery handwriting, it read: *'The Night Train' by Ellen Oppenheim*. He'd been right, his nan had written the piece of music. Did that mean she'd been responsible for everything that had happened since it had started playing?

Elliot held the tape and stared at the words. Had everything that just happened been a dream? No, he'd had no idea it was called 'The Night Train' when his mum had put it on. Whatever this tape was, it was special.

His mum threw open the door to her son's bedroom. She seemed surprised to find him standing there, holding the tape in his hand and staring at it as though it was an incomprehensible piece of technology.

'Oh, poppet,' she said, pulling him into a warm, slightly damp hug. She smelled how she always smelled: like a mixture of honey nut cereal and printer ink. It was a smell that told Elliot he really was home this time. 'Did you manage to get some sleep?' his mum asked, holding him at arm's length.

Elliot nodded. 'Sort of,' he said.

'I know exactly what you mean.'

He smiled at her. He was almost completely sure that she had no idea what he meant, but he wasn't going to start trying to explain that he'd spent the night with a dragon, adventuring through Grandma Ellen's memories. Besides, he wasn't even sure if any of it had been real. The longer he was awake, the less possible any of it seemed.

'Can I ask you something?' said Elliot.

'Of course you can, poppet.'

He took a deep breath. 'What happened to Grandma Ellen's nans?'

Mum took a seat on the edge of Elliot's bed. 'Funny you should ask,' said his mum, looking at him curiously. 'One of them we never knew because her father was adopted. But the other . . . we always said we'd wait until you were a bit older to tell you. It's a bit of a sad story, though I suppose you know a little something about sadness now already.' She paused as though she was afraid of what she was about to say. 'Your great-great-grandma was on the *Titanic* when it sank.'

'Was she really?'

Mum nodded. 'She managed to find a place on a lifeboat, but hypothermia set in later and she didn't make it.' Elliot took a moment to remember the gentle smile of the woman on the boat. 'Your poor nan never got to have her own nan. It's a shame; from what her mother told her she was a wonderful woman. A poet and a musician. Apparently, she used to tell jokes, too. Jokes so funny they made people pee themselves.'

'Where were they from?'

'Her family were originally from Austria, I think, though they moved to England a long time ago.'

'Why did Grandma Ellen never tell me?' he asked.

'I think there were lots of things she wanted to tell you,' said his mum. 'Your nan was always just waiting for the right time.' She stood up and clapped her hands together, trying her best to look chirpy. 'Right,' she said. 'Shall we have pancakes for breakfast?'

'Yes, please,' said Elliot, whose belly was making sounds like a dishwasher.

As she was leaving his room, Elliot's mum turned and looked him over. She frowned. Elliot looked down at himself too. He realised he was still wearing the clothes that the conductor had given him after he'd fallen into the mud in Latvia. He'd completely forgotten that he'd managed to lose his entire school uniform.

'I won't ask why you're dressed like a character from *Jumanji*,' said his mum. 'But I would like you to be dressed properly for school in five minutes.'

Elliot nodded nervously.

What was he going to do?

Once she'd left the room, he flung open the drawers of his wardrobe, half-expecting to see rain falling on to a train platform.

But there was no rain.

There were pants and socks in a canvas box, most of them full of holes. There were T-shirts folded in a stack, most of them from concerts. And there was his school uniform, hanging from a hook, perfectly washed and smelling like the rose garden of a seaside cottage. Elliot shook the trousers and shirt out on to the bed. Both looked as good as new, their patches and stitches, stains and creases all vanished without a trace.

'Thank you,' said Elliot, hoping that his words would somehow find the tall conductor.

On the bus to school, tired and full of pancakes, Elliot wore his earphones. He listened to all the songs he'd been missing over the previous weeks. He listened to The Dubliners and Kraftwerk and Slipknot. He listened to old recordings of his nan. He listened to Ludwig van Beethoven, performed by people who were born hundreds of years after he'd died.

Until he felt someone tugging gently at his elbow.

It was Lewis.

'What are you listening to?' he asked. 'I can hear it from the other side of the bus.'

Elliot tugged one earphone out of one ear.

'It's Beethoven,' he said. 'Sorry, I'll turn it down.'

'That's okay,' said Lewis, dropping into the seat next to Elliot. 'Is that the dead guy? It's like classical music, right? Mum said she played it to me while she was pregnant. She said she thought it would make me smart but I still can't say my favourite foods in Spanish so I don't know if it worked.'

Elliot passed the earphone over to Lewis, who looked surprised to be offered it. Elliot tried his best to smile. Once he'd realised that Elliot wasn't going to shout at him again, Lewis accepted the earphone and jammed it into his ear.

The two boys listened to Beethoven as the bus wound its way through the quiet streets. At rusty, graffiti-covered shelters, other kids waited in huddles.

They climbed on to the bus, shouting and squawking and singing and laughing, all of them clutching phones that showed videos of people falling off skateboards and cats climbing over giggling babies.

The bus passed the corner shop.

And the Indian restaurant.

And the boarded-up pub.

'Isn't it weird,' said Elliot, 'how music makes everything look different?'

'Yeah,' said Lewis. 'It makes everything feel like in films.'

Lewis stomped his foot loudly against the floor of the bus in time with the music. He was out of time, but Elliot didn't mind. A group of older kids who'd just got on to the bus gave them funny looks. Lewis scowled back at them until they turned away.

'Is it true your nan died?' Lewis asked.

'Yeah,' said Elliot.

'That sucks,' said Lewis.

'I know,' said Elliot.

'My hamster died once,' said Lewis. 'It's not as a big as a nan, but I was still sad.'

'I've never seen a hamster,' Elliot explained. 'Except on TV.'

'If you want, you can come over and see mine one day. Not the dead one – we buried that in our garden. In an Oreos box. My little sister loves Oreos. Mum says if she eats any more, she'll turn into one.'

When breaktime came, Elliot didn't hide in the toilet. He went to his violin lesson, out in the windy huts that surrounded the school. Mrs Lancet asked if he'd been practising. Elliot blushed, stared at his shoes and admitted he hadn't. His teacher told him not to worry.

'Music,' she told him, 'is not a chore. If you want to get better, play more. If you don't, don't worry about it.'

Elliot assured her that it never felt like a chore and that he did want to get better. He asked if they might be able to learn a certain piece by a certain long-dead composer from Germany. It was the grade above what Elliot was playing at the moment, pointed out Mrs Lancet. It would be difficult. Really difficult. Elliot said he would put in as much time as it took.

After that, the day unwound, long and slow. It was the kind of day you spent staring out of windows, wishing you could be charging across the field or falling asleep in the shadow of a willow tree. Everyone was restless and sweaty and incredibly uninterested in how to multiply fractions or figure out where to put apostrophes.

When his mum came to collect Elliot from school, she was dressed in a long, black dress, with a wide, black hat perched on top of her head. Elliot had never seen his mum wear so much black before. It was as though she was wearing a Halloween costume.

'You're only supposed to wear black,' she whispered to Elliot as he climbed into the car. 'But I couldn't face going the whole hog.' Elliot realised that his mum was wearing boots that were as yellow as sunflowers.

'Do I have to wear black too?' asked Elliot.

His mum looked at him curiously for a moment. She was thinking. 'No,' she said, finally. 'No, you can wear whatever you want.' She smiled at him. 'Your nan would have wanted you to wear whatever makes you happiest. Let's pop home and get you changed.'

23

At home, Elliot changed into a pair of loose, lime-green shorts and the T-shirt from the band Good Charlotte. It had come from the very first concert he'd gone to with Grandma Ellen. When she'd said he could buy a shirt, he'd purposely chosen one so big that he would never grow out of it. Four years later, it still looked more like a dress than a top. It hung past his knees.

Together, Elliot and his mum got into the car and drove. He soon realised they weren't heading for the church. Instead, they looped around by the school, passed the corner shop and pulled up outside a small, red-brick bungalow, with a sloping roof. The flowerbeds in its front garden were overgrown and some of the petals on the flowers had turned the burnt colour of old book pages.

It was his nan's house.

Elliot looked through the window at it and felt a wave of sadness rush over him like cold water. He'd spent countless afternoons at that house, watching the music channel, playing the piano, doing jigsaw puzzles and singing in the garden.

'Why are we at Nan's house?' Elliot asked quietly.

'Well,' said his mum. 'Since Nan isn't with us any more, it's our house now. And we'll need to decide what to do with it.'

Elliot hadn't even thought about what would happen to the house yet. He supposed he thought it would just stand empty but, of course, that wouldn't be the case. When someone left a house, someone new always moved in.

His mum reached out a hand and squeezed Elliot's shoulder. 'I know it's hard,' she said. 'I know you two were so incredibly close, and I know part of that was because I was always so busy. You went to Nan after school because I was working, and you spent so many weekends with her because I was always sent away to report on something.'

'I liked going on trips with Nan.'

'I know you did, poppet. And I know that no one

will ever replace your nan, not for you and not for me, but if we decide to live here, then it would mean I could work less because we wouldn't be paying rent. We'd get to spend more time together. I'd be here when you got back from school and I'd be here at weekends so we could go on adventures.'

Elliot's eyes grew wide with surprise. 'You mean, we could actually move in here?'

'Well, would you like to?'

Elliot took a moment to think.

Moving into Grandma's house would mean the opposite of trying to hide from his memories of her. She'd be everywhere: in the garden, in the kitchen, doing a crossword by the TV. And sometimes it would hurt, but it already hurt anyway. Of course it would. It always hurt whenever something wonderful ended. But it wouldn't really be over, and plus it would mean he could be with his mum. He could show her all the things his nan had shown him, and take her to all the places they'd gone, and play her all the music they'd loved.

Eyes full to the brim with tears, Elliot turned to his mum and nodded. 'I think I'd like to live there,' he said. 'Then she'll always be close by.'

His mum hugged him and held on for a very long

time, until she realised they were going to be late.

*

As he walked into the church, holding his mum's hand, Elliot was amazed to see how crowded it was. The seats were packed with people who'd come to say goodbye to Grandma Ellen. In fact, so many people had come for the funeral that groups of people in black coats were forced to stand at the back and the side. A surprising number of them had done what Elliot's mum had done. There were pink flowers pushed through buttonholes, red handkerchiefs tied around necks and green hats perched on heads.

At the front of the church lay a long, polished coffin, with gleaming brass handles. Elliot tried not to think about what was inside it. The idea made him want to run out of the church and throw up.

Elliot and his mum took seats on the hard, wooden pews at the very front. Mum put her canvas work bag down between them. Why, he wondered, would his mum bring her work bag to the funeral?

He snuck a glance and spotted a piece of green fabric poking out of the top.

'There's something sticking out of your bag,' he whispered.

'Oh,' said Mum. 'That's just one of my old toys. It's silly really, but I like keeping it around. Your nan gave it to me, back when I was little. She said he'd look after me.' Mum opened her bag slightly so that Elliot could look inside. He let out a squeal of surprise. Inside his mum's bag, looking slightly dishevelled, stained and chewed, was Kimorin. The same stuffed, floppy Kimorin that the girl had been clutching in Bourton-on-the-Water. It was, without a doubt, the same little dragon he'd spent the night sharing a train carriage with.

'I ought to give him to you, really,' said Mum. 'I'm too old for him now.'

'No,' said Elliot. 'You should keep him, Mum. At least for today.'

He felt his mum's arm slip around his shoulders. She pressed a tissue into his hand and he used it to blow his nose. Seconds later, she burst into sobs too. Elliot tried to wipe some of the snot off the tissue before passing it back over to her. His mum laughed so loudly that everyone in the church turned to stare.

The vicar climbed the steps up to his lectern. He wore a flowing white robe and had bristly, grey eyebrows so thick they almost hung over his eyes.

Everyone stood up. Lifting his hands in welcome, the vicar explained that they were gathered together to celebrate the life of Ellen Oppenheim, who had been born on 15 August 1933. He said he was thrilled but not surprised to see that Ellen had touched so many lives, and then asked everyone who could find a seat to sit back down.

The vicar talked about how much of a long, interesting and wonderful life Grandma Ellen had led. How she'd been a cellist who was known around the world and how she'd been a friend to people in every place she'd ever visited. How she'd worked as a nurse for some years in the seventies. How she'd spent a year travelling with the fair, selling tickets for the carousel and living off candyfloss and hot dogs. All around him, Elliot heard people trying not to cry. His mum pulled out more tissues and passed them around. Stained-glass windows painted the stone floor in bright colours.

He talked about how she volunteered at the shelter for homeless people, and how much everyone was going to miss the rich, gooey brownies she baked in the winter. How she'd been such a good friend to him, personally, when he'd got sick and couldn't go shopping for himself. He talked about how she'd met her husband, Pawel, when she'd been travelling across Europe with her orchestra.

He said he could remember one evening, during the coldest Christmas they'd ever had, when he'd gone to visit her and found a squirrel in her living room. Grandma Ellen had told him that she was worried it was too cold for it outside. She'd set up a little nest for the squirrel under the living room table and had been feeding it milky tea and pistachio nuts.

Everyone giggled.

'And now,' said the vicar, 'we're going to hear a piece of music played by Ellen's grandson, Elliot.'

When his mum had first asked Elliot to play something at the funeral, he'd said yes, but meant no. He'd come up with all kinds of ways to get out of having to do it. He'd pretend to be sick; he'd smash his violin; he'd run away. There was no way he was ever going to stand up in front of so many people and play. What would be the point? It wasn't going to bring Grandma Ellen back. She wouldn't even be able to hear it.

But now he was doing exactly that.

Because that was what his grandmother had done.

And her grandmother.

And all their grandparents, all the way back in time.

Trembling, he stood before the church full of people and lifted his violin out of its case.

The dragon's words came back to him: *It's only goodbye if you forget.*

And he wouldn't forget.

Not in a week or a month or a year or a hundred years.

As he played, Elliot knew Grandma Ellen was there. Not in the big, wooden box, standing at the front of the church, but in the music. The music that Beethoven wrote as a scared child, the music that the band played as the *Titanic* sank, the music that the Hush-Hushes sang in their cave. Elliot understood that the music was his connection to the universe; it tied him to the future, to the past and to the present. It tied him to Grandma Ellen and his great-grandpa and all the people standing in front of him. The sound lifted them outside of time. It took them up past the houses and the streets and the cars, to the place where they'd come from and the place where they'd go. And it wasn't scary. And it wasn't sad. It was just . . . everything. And everything was okay.

EPILOGUE

Rehearsals had gone on far later than usual. The musicians of the Grand Oak Theatre were exhausted. They were preparing for a show that was due to open in three days. Three nights from now, every seat in the audience would be taken. The dancers would have to dance and the orchestra would have to play, regardless of whether they felt ready or not.

Finally, after what felt like for ever, the conductor told the musicians to head home.

'Everyone except for Elliot,' she announced. 'Elliot, could you please hang back so that we can have a chat?'

He tried not to look too annoyed as he watched each of his friends pack away their instruments and leave. He had no idea what Sarah Tuppett wanted to talk to him about. Maybe, he thought, she was going to tell him off for keeping a secret stash of wine gums in his pocket and chomping on them whenever there was a break in practice.

It turned out that Sarah Tuppett actually wanted to discuss how they ought to end the last song of the show. As she was going over the possibilities, Elliot couldn't help wondering why she was asking for his advice. She was the conductor; didn't she know much better than him what they ought to do?

After what felt like an hour, Sarah let him go. He packed his violin into its case and shrugged on his old coat. Elliot wondered whether he ought to take a pod home, but decided not to. It was a peaceful night and he could do with a walk after spending the entire day in an uncomfortable plastic chair.

He took the shortcut, out of the theatre's back door and across the train station. He paid no attention to the thousands of floating adverts that followed him as he went. Things were quiet. Things were generally quiet on weekdays, with most people working at computers in their homes. It was only on weekends when the streets and stations filled up with people getting together to relax.

The closer he got to the pub, the more Elliot wished he could go straight home and fall into bed. But it wasn't an option. He'd promised to meet a friend for a catch-up. The friend was an old one who he knew from school and he was visiting town for a few days from France.

Elliot pushed open the door to The Merman.

It was completely empty.

Not a single person in sight.

'Hello?' he called out. 'Is anyone there?'

He considered going home anyway. But before he could turn around, everyone Elliot Oppenheim knew jumped out and started singing 'Happy Birthday'.

Elliot started to laugh and couldn't stop. He felt the hands of his friends clapping him on the back. He'd completely and utterly forgotten that it was his birthday. They'd all been so lost in the preparation for the show that it had been like nothing else existed.

Someone turned out the lights and a cake appeared, with thirty burning candles sticking out of it. Elliot counted them with shock. Could he really be thirty already? Hadn't he turned twenty just the other day? Where had all the years gone?

'Close your eyes and make a wish,' said Emma, the tuba player from the orchestra.

'Yeah, shut 'em, Oppenheim,' said the flautist.

'Or your wish won't come true.'

Elliot did as he was told.

He sucked in a deep breath.

He made a wish.

And he blew.

Someone turned the lights back on and Elliot opened his eyes. Ribbons of smoke curled out of the candles. Everyone was cheering. Elliot realised that it wasn't just the orchestra or his friends from music college, but Lewis and Mrs Lancet and his mum were there too.

But Elliot was distracted by something.

At the back of the pub, deep in conversation, stood a boy and a dragon. The boy was dressed like an explorer and the dragon was wearing a straw hat. They both looked utterly lost and out of place. The boy stood with his feet turned inward and the dragon was beaming.

The boy was familiar. The boy was . . .

Elliot blinked again. They'd disappeared. Of course they'd disappeared. Because they hadn't really been there. That would have been impossible.

'You okay, mate?' asked the clarinettist, passing him a slice of cake.

'Just a little tired,' said Elliot.

'Aren't we all?' said Sarah Tuppett. 'But soon enough, the curtains shall close, and we will be free folk once again!'

'Until the next show,' muttered the percussionist.

Elliot stared at the space where the boy and the dragon had been standing a second before. They'd looked so real. Why, of all things, would he imagine that?

'None of you invited a dragon, did you?' he asked. 'Or a boy?'

'You really are tired,' said Sarah. 'Remind me not to work you so hard.'

And so began a long night of loud music and terrible dancing. Old friends caught up, new friends were made, and cake was eaten. It was a truly successful surprise party and a birthday that would not be forgotten in a hurry.

By the time he got home, Elliot was shattered. He put away his violin, climbed into his pyjamas and rolled into bed.

As he lay on his back, staring up at the ceiling, he thought about Grandma Ellen. What would she think if she could see him now, getting ready to perform with an orchestra for a month of performances in a giant theatre? She'd be proud, he knew that. She'd probably come to every one of the show's performances, sitting at the very front, with a Grand Oak T-shirt on and a Thermos of tea in her hand.

He wished he'd been able to introduce her to all of his friends from the orchestra. Elliot knew they'd like her as much as she'd like them.

He had a thought.

Tired as he was, Elliot got out of bed, dashed downstairs and slid a small wooden chest off his bookshelf. It was a place that he used to keep small objects that meant a lot to him. Over the years, it had grown pretty full. There were tickets from concerts, Polaroid photographs of friends, scraps of sheet music, souvenir coins, luggage tags, business cards, uneaten sweets and all kinds of other little things that might look meaningless to anyone else but him.

He dug through the objects until he found what he was looking for.

A tape.

He had a bit of trouble finding a tape player (who listened to tapes any more?) but he eventually discovered one at the very back of the attic, hiding under a thick layer of dust and a pile of folk records that he'd bought at a jumble sale.

Back in his bed, Elliot got under the covers and listened to 'The Night Train' by Ellen Oppenheim. It began with four notes, played on a cello. The four notes swayed gently, playing over and over in a loop. They gradually picked up speed, tumbling together into a melody that took hold of Elliot.

The song conjured memories of Grandma Ellen so easily it was like watching a film. He saw her in the garden, whistling back to the magpies. He saw her face split into a smile as he perfected a bar of Beethoven. He saw her holding him to her chest as she beat a path through a rowdy crowd to get them to the front of a concert.

She felt so close.

Hours later, Elliot woke up.

It was the middle of the night and a little dragon

was bouncing happily on the edge of his bed.

'Blimey, Olio,' said Kimorin, the glowing lantern swinging from his tail. 'You ain't stayed small, have you?'

Elliot didn't know what to say.

From inside his wardrobe came the sound of a whistling train. 'We gonna catch that thing or not?' asked the dragon, holding out an envelope. 'I got your ticket right here.'

Acknowledgements

★ ★ *★*

A book like this one might start with a person typing alone in a room, but it only reaches you with a lot of help from a lot of different people. So I'd very much like to thank Nazima, Laura, Tig, Michelle, Joana, and everyone else at Hachette Children's Group for all their hard work.

I'd also like to thank George for bringing the story to life with his pictures, yet again. And I'd like to thank Renata and Mischa for putting up with me at home. Of course, I'd also like to thank my grandma and grampy, who I miss very much, as you can probably imagine.

BEN BROOKS

FROM THE AUTHOR OF
STORIES FOR BOYS WHO DARE TO BE DIFFERENT

THE
GREATEST
INVENTOR

HE'S THEIR ONLY HOPE. HE'S ... NOT WHAT THEY EXPECTED.